www.tredition.de

AF197109

Stefan Prebil works and writes in his alp cottage high above Lake Brienz.

After a career in top management around the globe, his work today consists of consulting companies in the technology sector, coaching and - in writing novels.

His stories deal with personal relationships, extraordinary biographies, in the context of social developments and rapid technological progress.

.

Stefan Prebil

Ramey Rieger

ICEDIAMONDS

VOLUME I

WHO FAILS TO HONOR,

WILL BE HUMBLED

www.tredition.de

© 2019 Stefan Prebil
Cover, illustration: Stefan Prebil
Cover picture: Adobe Stock License

Translation and   Ramey Rieger
proofreading:

Publishing & Printing: tredition GmbH, Halenreie
                        40-44, 22359 Hamburg

ISBN
Paperback   978-3-7497-9660-1
Hardcover   978-3-7497-9661-8
e-Book   978-3-7497-9662-5

Content

ONE

Comfortably seated in Business Class, Sam turns aside and presses his face against the oval window, eager for a better view. The thrumming beneath his feet alerted him to the pilot opening the landing flaps. Once an avid private pilot himself, he knows what comes next.

The machine will decelerate, slightly bucking and weaving. Then a powerful, jolting shudder. Landing lights illuminate a thick stream of incandescent snowflakes. From where he is sitting, visibility just makes it to the engine. Beyond that, red blinking smudges hint at navigation lights on the wing tips. Clacking sounds below tell Sam that the landing gear is moving into place. Like a seasoned mustang tamer, the Icelandair pilot gives his machine just enough rein to buck and rear until she succumbs to his dominant will and is firmly guided onto the runway. Sam assumes the pilot is accustomed to much wilder weather.

The cabin lights are dimmed. "Cabin crew take your seats – landing in five minutes," the pilot's taciturn voice buzzes over the speakers. Sam recognizes the foreigners on board by the occasional squeals and whispered prayers, while the Icelandic couple across from him pays no mind to the prancing plane. Their conversation is much more interesting. Sam grins, remembering the in-flight magazine boast, "Welcome to the second windiest country on the planet! The windiest is uninhabited."

He gazes out dreamily at the swaying machine before snatching up the Heineken can from the broad tray beside him and considering it intently.

Aluminum. The engine aperture's aluminum cannot be warmer than sixty degrees below zero but bears the punishment without flinching. Flying at an altitude of more than ten kilometers, the pressure drop causes the cabin to expand by about five centimeters. Upon descent, it shrinks back to its original size. Passengers are oblivious to the change, feeling utterly secure in a thin aluminum tube as they race through rarefied air at over a thousand kilometers per hour, drinking espresso, watching films, snuggling into their blankets. As long, of course, as the flight runs smoothly.

Ignorance is bliss. The rare accident happens to other people, no need to worry. Unless, as now, the elements demonstrate their power.

Sam turns to his neighbor, an impish grin on his face, and softly implies, "Hardly a person on board is aware that a mere two millimeters of aluminum hold this plane together. Two millimeters separating safe and warm from frozen death. Good to know we would die painlessly."

The man glanced up from his book, casting a brief look past Sam to the window before replying with casual superiority, "Fragile as that may sound, disasters are rare occurrences; technology and materials are far too sophisticated. And what makes you think we wouldn't feel a thing? I wouldn't count on it. We are flying at approximately two hundred and fifty kilometers per hour; it is about zero degrees outside and we are low enough for plenty of oxygen. So even if the cabin suddenly bursts, we will die knowing it."

Nodding appreciatively, Sam studies his neighbor more closely. A reedy build encased in a coarsely knit wool sweater. Judging by his polished elocution, a German. What is he reading? Digital transformation based on low code programming. Aha, a nerd.

The plane takes a mighty blow and Sam is lifted a few millimeters out of his seat, enough to feel a breeze passing through. He sees his neighbor clutch the armrest frantically, his knuckles turning white.

Sam drains his beer in one go, tightening his fist around the empty can. Twisting and pressing the aluminum noisily into a flat disk, he drops it next to the one he crushed earlier. He had boarded the plane to Iceland with the intention of curbing his alarming drinking habit. But when he declined lunch, the cool blonde stewardess winked and placed a second beer in front of him. So much for one last beer.

What of it? Grinning, he nods to his blurred mirror image in the window. His life thus far has not been a paradigm of discipline and firm resolve. Taken with his tendency to make impulsive decisions, he is accustomed to causing a fracas, intentionally or not.

Snow at the end of April – that'll up the challenge and adventure he muses as the machine continues to plow through gusting air.

Butterflies. Some are his doubts that he is physically fit enough to do the job. The rest of them are simply his boyish anticipation to find out just that.

At his send-off last week, his colleagues heartily raised their glasses to their departing boss, kindly congratulating him on his audacious plans. He is fifty-five, a well-established manager with a lucrative job, and was giving it all up to be a diving guide in Iceland.

Five years ago, he told them, he had fulfilled a youthful dream and become a diving instructor. It is now time he put it to use, to seek new inspiration and to pass his responsibilities on to the next generation. The last with a wink at the young personnel candidate who is most likely to take his place. The truth is, he has only been there a year and is already bored out of his mind.

Their faces told him what they really thought: Look at Mr. Moneybags, tired of his new toy! Now he's off to his next egocentric frolic while we're stuck here, hanging onto our jobs and trying to make ends meet.

He could care less and had no issues with what went unsaid. He is well aware that he has simply exchanged money and power for life and self-fulfillment. The hunger is the same. And so are his methods. He is just as willing to selfishly sacrifice relationships and friends or leave employees to their fate.

He, Samuel Frei, had worked his way up from pharmaceutical salesclerk to CEO of multinational corporations, he and no other, was Magic Sam. After years of brilliant success, enduring the intrigues, the immense pressure to make profits, his increasingly unconscionable ego and subsequently battered and shattered marriage, he brilliantly failed.

His career took a dive. He wasn't much surprised. Stress had taken him to the bottle more often than not. In his cups, he was convinced it would eventually come to light that he was not all he was made out to be. He was an imposter. After the fall, he hired himself out as an interim manager for smaller businesses. His clients were sophisticated and paid handsomely, but they could not heal the festering wounds inflicted by his failure.

Three months ago, a diving buddy asked him if he wanted to join him in Iceland, working as a guide. He himself had signed on for 2,000€ a month. They would only be diving every other day or so with tourists. Usually snorkeling tours in dry suits. But, hey, the Silfra Crack! Floating in icy, crystal-clear waters directly between the Eurasian and American continental plates, it's breathtaking. As are the country and its people.

Sam googled the location and was immediately hot to trot. He applied to every diving school in Reykjavik and got a job as a guide. The monthly pay was less than what he usually earned in a day. Who cares? He has a year's worth of fuck you money and is utterly fed up.

Before starting the job, he had to take a course in dry suit diving. He had diddled a bit on his applications, misleading potential employers. He claimed that, being Swiss, he had plenty of diving experience in icy water. In truth, he has never worked with this equipment before. Filling in the knowledge gaps and fitting himself out with the required gear was child's play. Not so easy to plug up is his lack of experience. He would be expected to lead several groups a day through very cold water. That takes stamina, both mental and physical, and he is not sure he has either. He will just have to wing it. If he blew it, he could always flee to his cottage in the Alps.

Thundering onto the runaway, the plane touches down in Keflavik International Airport, shaking Sam from his reverie. Engaging thrust reversal, the aircraft shudders and slows, skidding over the snow toward the terminal.

The pilots, two young, blond and bearded Vikings, stand at the cockpit door, thanking the passengers as they debarked, wishing them a nice weekend. "You, too!" Sam responds with an urbane grin, taking one last look at the pretty stewardess, "nice job!"

His grin broadens as he collects his two enormous trolley cases stuffed with gear and clothing and tromps off to customs to the sound of his combat boots resounding over the tiles.

TWO

S am shoots up from the rickety IKEA bed, once again dislodging several slats beneath the thin mattress. His butt promptly succumbs to gravity, leaving him wedged in the gulf. Cursing and flailing, he manages to liberate himself and reach for his cellphone, only to plop back onto the sagging bed. 5:30 am. He still has fifteen minutes until he has to leave for the diving shop with his colleagues. They have the first shift. He is still having trouble adjusting to the nearly endless Icelandic sunlight. Now, at the end of May, the sun shines until 2 am. There is a short twilight between 2 and 3 am and at 5 am the sun is already so high again you'd think it was ten.

***

Three weeks ago, Silfra Scuba's personnel director Yana collected him at the airport and brought him to his room at Vatnagarðar 18 in Reykjavik.

Shortened to V18 by its inhabitants, the building had once housed offices before his tour company bought it and converted it into a kind of dormitory for their guides. V18 is located in an industrial zone on the outskirts of Reykjavik, directly across from the container harbor. Downtown Reykjavik is an hour's march on foot, but there is a bus running along the turnpike directly behind the house. Summer is truly short in Iceland and must be exploited to the hilt, so the streets and harbor are full of activity nearly twenty-four hours a day.

Despite the constant noise, Sam is glad he garnered a room at the front of the building with a window. There's about sixty people in the house and all of them work for Iceland Adventure, Silfra Scuba's parent company, and some of them are closeted in interior, windowless rooms. No daylight, no fresh air, their biorhythm determined by the sound of in-coming shift workers showering and cooking in the communal kitchen, loudly trying to one-up each other with anecdotes about the day's incredibly scatterbrained clients. Each day, endlessly revolving shifts of mountain guides, drivers, dinghy captains and diving guides tramp in and out of V18. The first teams set off at six in the morning and the last return around midnight. Summer tourists in Iceland also keep long hours.

Adjusting to conditions of dormitory life, as he refers to it, had taken him a while. At fifty-five, he is more than twice the age of the average resident and has, over the years, developed distinct habits and concepts of cohabitation. These are not necessarily shared by the younger generation. There are three showers for twenty women and the same number for forty men. Hot water in Iceland smells like sulfur, being pumped directly from geothermic boreholes. Sam has no problem with the smell, but the showers' hygiene level is a challenge indeed. He adopted the habit of wearing his flipflops to and in the showers to avoid direct contact with the hair, soap residue and other ominous fluids coating the shower stall floor.

Otherwise, within the month he had adapted well to life and work in Iceland. Relieved to relinquish his managerial mask, he is happy to keep his opinion on the diving shop's structural shortcomings to himself. All diving instructors, regardless of gender, have bloated egos. Perhaps it is a matter of being driven to prove themselves, having come to the profession as a last resort after failing elsewhere? Or maybe it's their nonconformist pride as free spirits traveling the world in search of the ultimate diving spot, much more eclectic than the simple sheep they herd? Whatever. Each and every one of them believes they know better than the others. Sam discovered this idiosyncrasy during his training in Thailand. Accustomed to being the know-it-all, he objected to his teachers' know-even-more condescension and provoked more than one cockfight. Here, though, he finds it gratifying to readily submit to lectures and to humbly bow down to the alpha male or female of the day.

He has their respect and that is enough. He is closemouthed when it comes to his executive past, his advanced age is suspicious enough. Most of his colleagues are somewhere between early twenties and early thirties.

The only other exception is Ilias. A white-bearded Greek, Ilias had high-tailed it to Iceland to get his cut of the highest diving instructor wages in the world. Two thousand euros a month plus lodging is more than twice as much as paid elsewhere. It turns out though, that the wages are so high due to Iceland's exorbitant cost of living. Sam soon discovered that they are only getting the required minimum wage, less than what a supermarket cashier earns. None of Sam's colleagues seem to mind, though. Many are there to save money for other ventures when the season in Iceland closes. They are adept at frugality. And Ilias is truly spartan.

A couple years back, Ilias had fulfilled a lifelong dream and opened a diving shop in Thailand. Not an easy undertaking since commercial law requires the greater share of all foreign enterprises – at least fifty-one percent – to be held in native hands. Risky business for foreigners, which is why most of them partner up with Thai trustee operations, relying on contract fidelity. Others, as was the case with Ilias, rely on fidelity of the heart. He was truly besotted with his lady partner, Phat.

And business boomed. Attracting not only eager tourists, but covetous racketeers as well. Not long, and the local mobsters turned up, wanting their portion of the pie in exchange for services rendered, including their private version of fire insurance. It would be a crying shame to see the lovely diving shop burned to the ground. Phat knew her country's customs and urged Ilias to pay and be done with it, but he refused. His European ethics cost him both his love and his livelihood. Especially when Phat offered to buy him out for a tenth of what the place was worth, which Ilias also turned down, pained and offended.

Things came to a head when the mob told him flat out that he would not be the first foreigner to have a diving accident, his body washed up on some unknown shore. Shark bait. Ilias fled the country he loved with nothing more than the clothes on his back.

The story came out one night while Sam and Ilias were having a couple beers together. It was a rare occasion. Otherwise exceedingly close-mouthed, the Greek cooks his meals and sits alone on the dilapidated sofa in the hallway, eating in grim determination. He will stick out the summer, save as much as he can, return to Thailand and start afresh. Nothing else interests him. He would leave today, if he had the cash.

The two older men share a shelf in one of the refrigerators posted around the tables like massive sentries. Each resident has a shelf for their supplies, marked with their names. Beer, a veritable luxury at five euros a can, is better kept in your room or hung outside, if you are lucky enough to have a window. Otherwise, it's gone. When a higher percentage of alcohol is desired, beer is mixed with Brennivín, Icelandic firewater, both of which can only be bought at Vínbúðin, state-owned liquor stores. For many years, beer was banned from Iceland. The result is a country of liquor drinkers.

If you cook your own food, keeping to a mono-diet of cheap pasta, and imbibe a minimum of alcohol, you can live well on ten euros a day. The first week or two, Sam took the bus and ate downtown. Unlike most of his colleagues, he can afford such luxuries. But he eventually lost his taste for thirty-euro burgers and eating alone. He resorted to stockpiling frozen Asian convenience foods and, for diversity, picking up an occasional pizza from the gas station across the turnpike from V18. Now, he 'cooks' his frozen cardboard dishes in the microwave, usually joining his teammates at the table.

For the umpteenth time, Sam lifts his mattress and reinstates the escaped slats. Burning thirst and queasiness remind him of the barbecue last night. Pulling up the blinds with one hand, he grabs a carton of orange juice from the flimsy shelf next to his bed with the other. For a moment he watches shredded clouds whip over the bay and shrilly tooting cranes shift containers from here to there. Beyond the bay, clouds have gathered at Esja's pinnacle and it looks like it's raining up there. Locals speak of the nine-hundred-fourteen-meter-high mountain as if it is a dear house pet. It is just another day. It could be worse. It could be yesterday.

V18 squats in the center of an industrial area, surrounded by wind and weather-beaten car repair shops and warehouses. Behind the dilapidated dormitory is an emergency exit opening onto a spacious concrete slab, on the edge of which is a fire escape leading down to the access road below. This barren terrace is where the diving teams meet once a week to grill sausages, drink beer and recap the week's tours.

On the side facing the road embankment, wild lupines abound, the same flowers that magically color the summer-green volcanos a gentle violet. On the other side, they are entertained by the bustling container harbor and heavy grey ocean. Someone had found a few plastic chairs long past their prime and installed them on the terrace. Another someone had scrounged up a couple of trestle tables and benches. Their grill consists of concrete blocks with twisted, rusting reinforcing bars.

And yet, sit there at two in the morning with sunglasses firmly in place. Watch the perpetual wind whip lathered clouds across the sky and mottle the low-lying sun. Bathing in ever-shifting, ethereal and spectacular light, you find yourself on another planet altogether.

Yesterday evening, Sam joined the others around ten. As usual, Chuck was sprawled in his deck chair, sun-bathing in t-shirt and shorts by fourteen degrees Celsius, regaling them with his British humor and laughing loudest at his own jokes. Spotting Sam, he put down his beer, brushed some long, black strands of hair from his face and went to get another chair. When he returned, he pulled Sam into a hug, patting him on the back and muttering: "It'll be okay, mate!" The next moment, he ladled potato salad and two sausages onto a plate, fished a can of beer from a tub, handed them to Sam and beckoned him to sit by his side. Jace, head down, eyes boring holes in the concrete while mechanically stroking his bushy red beard, occupied the chair on Sam's other side. Like Chuck, Jace is also British, but aside from their nationality's dedication to black humor, they have little in common. Chuck's stocky physique and aggressive nature puts one in mind of a pit bull. His polite, English veneer thinly masks his underlying unpredictability, ever ready for a wild brawl. Jace, on the other hand, is a tall, gangly man, his build typical of long-distance runners. He is sparing of words until beer loosens his tongue.

Emma, next to Jace, is leaning her lovely head on his shoulder. The two of them fell hard and deeply in love when they met here in Iceland. At twenty-two, with a bobbysoxer figure and countless freckles in a cheerful face, Emma was initially underestimated. But not for long. She is a masterful diving instructor and can be very firm when she has to be – such as when tourists hesitate to follow her safety instructions. Then, her kind eyes turn adamant and Sam gets a glimpse of an indomitable will lying just beneath inherent good cheer, girlish innocence or motherly tenderness, whichever is currently on the surface. An astonishingly multifaceted woman for her age and Sam sometimes wonders which is the true Emma. According to Jace, Emma is a loved child of well-situated parents, growing up with all the British upper-class privileges during her childhood on her family's estate. This would explain Emma's self-assurance as well as her clearly defined concepts of right and wrong. On anyone else her conservative ethics would seem arrogant amid the lax morality of a diving guide's adventurous lifestyle. Yet she is anything but snooty, sensing when to concede a point and her evident professionalism is rightfully admired. Emma's cheerful, outgoing nature is a good match for Jace's silent brooding. She even thinks to bring him sandwiches along for the tour each day.

Yesterday, Chuck and Sam were paired for the Silfra tour, along with Marie, a beautiful French woman Sam found extraordinarily attractive. She stood behind him now, gently massaging his shoulders.

"Don't worry, now, you didn't drown anyone. The two of us are fine, too. So, let's forget it about it and enjoy our beer," Chuck exclaimed and erupted in laughter.

"It could have been you," Sam teased Jace, who, although he wasn't directly involved, was taking things much more seriously. Sam gave his beard an amiable tug, earning a crooked smile. They clacked their beer cans and drank deeply.

Mickey and Julia joined them. He is another bearded, lanky Englishman; she a blond Ukrainian. They had met at the Great Barrier Reef some years ago and have been travelling the diving circuit together ever since. A few minutes later, Barbu and Simi turned up. The Romanian brothers had warmly welcomed Sam upon his arrival, going out of their way to show him around the dorm and diving shop.

Chuck challenged Sam with his eyes, spreading his arms wide and laughing. Everyone was waiting for him to tell them what really happened. Left with no choice, Sam began to recount the story, knowing full well that Chuck had already given his version and that word had spread like wildfire before the threesome had even gotten back to V18. He was also aware of how quickly the facts would be twisted, embellished and posted on every social media platform on the web. So, he was glad to tell it from his perspective.

Finishing his narrative, he looked up to find Drake and Tara, the diving shop managers, standing in front of him. Sam rose like a guilty child and found himself hugged by first one then the other.

"Well, have you rejoined the warm-blooded community? Is your body temperature back to normal?" Drake teased Sam. Tara added, "How are you handling the shock?" Sam's response was a shrug and a smile. Chuck gave his stock impudent grin; he was beyond the need for such reassurances.

Sam had met Drake for the first time during his instructor training in Thailand. An experienced diving manager and attractive Englishman in his mid-forties, Drake has traveled the world. He could easily be Clint Eastwood's twin, thinning hair and all. Especially his eyes, a sparkling grey, lit up when he spoke while rolling an omnipresent, unlit cigarillo around in his mouth. Sam has never seen him with a woman. Once in Thailand, when Drake went to pay for a round of drinks and left his wallet open on the table, he saw a picture of a woman and three children. Sam wanted to ask about the photograph, but a warning glance from Drake held him back. Sam believed he saw pain in that look. Like so many professional divers, Drake seemed to have little talent for settling down. Perhaps, that was what made them diving nomads in the first place.

Drake and Tara share Silfra Scuba management, an almost twenty-four-hour job on seven days of the week. Inquiries come from everywhere on the planet and reservations are slotted into six shifts with a maximum of eight snorkelers or two divers per guide. Safety is an extremely high priority. There have been deaths in the past and Silfra was in danger of getting a reputation as a high-risk diving spot, thanks to social media posts. At their first briefing with the new diving guides, Drake had quoted the founders of Easy Jet, "If you are concerned about the cost of safety, think about the price of an accident."

Tara is a former nurse from Glasgow where she had been in charge of a hospice for incurable drug addicts. She has seen countless young people die agonizing deaths. Instead of despairing, she drew strength from her own life's possibilities. Not quite thirty years old, Tara is a circumspect, confident manager on top of even the most hectic situation. She's feisty and has a seemingly endless collection of off-color jokes she employs, using humor to deflate her guides' bloated egos. She only comes up to Sam's chest but when called for, will plant her fists on her expansive hips, whip her blond braids from her chest and make herself heard.

Both Tara and Drake were visibly relieved that the day's events were nothing worse than a close shave. Apparently, they had been exhaustively questioned by the authorities and felt the aftermath called for a case of beer and a visit to their employees.

Drake tapped two bottles together and the resulting ping was the signal for all of them to rise from their seats and retrieve a beer. Ian, the easygoing bear of a man at the grill rolled sausages out of the fire's heat and came over, too. With his mighty red beard, wild mane and eyes permanently twinkling, Ian was a giant version of Gimli, the dwarf in Lord of the Rings.

"We were lucky today," Drake began addressing his people, "things could have been much worse. As far as I can tell, Chuck and Sam did nothing wrong and reacted quickly, precisely and professionally. This only goes to show that even with the most comprehensive safety measures we cannot let down our guard, not for a second. You all know the rule: the first mistake is life threatening; the second mistake is fatal. In this case, we made no second mistake and I want to thank you for that! The good news is that the authorities are not going to shut us down, tomorrow we can carry on business as usual. Sam and Chuck, however, can only return to work when the authorities have completed their investigation. So, let's relax and enjoy the evening. Cheers!"

The night sun kept thoughts of sleep at bay, not to mention the ungodly clamor of tooting cranes and beeping forklifts as they unloaded a container ship directly next to V18. Still, Sam hadn't wholly recovered from the afternoon's hypothermia. Shortly after midnight he withdrew to his room, the level of alcohol in his blood ensuring a dreamless sleep.

***

05:45 – time to get moving! Sam slips into the borrowed, quilted overall. His is still hanging to dry at the shop. He ties his combat boots and dons his Gore-Tex jacket. Iceland's weather is phenomenally fickle; mild and warm one minute, freezing winds and snow flurries smack you in the face the next. A woolen cap completes the outfit and Sam is ready to go. He looks into the small mirrored tile stuck to the wall beside the door. Not bad at all. Maybe the rings under his eyes are a bit pronounced, but otherwise he cuts a good figure. He smiles at his reflection. In the kitchen, he takes a couple of bananas and chocolate bars from his shelf.

On his way to the kitchen he sees Chuck and Marie already sitting on the sofa, ready to go. Neither of them looks very spritely and they respond to Sam's energetic "g'morning" with unconvincing smiles as he sweeps past them. When Sam returns and stands expectantly in front of them, Chuck merely dangles the keys in front of himself. You drive.

The three of them get into the van. Reykjavik is quiet this Saturday morning, there is little traffic at the moment. Most Icelanders are still in bed or have only recently called it a night. The weekend is just getting underway and few events or parties get into gear before midnight.

Sam takes the coastal road past Harpa, the State Opera house, driving to the harbor district where the diving shop is situated. As he backs up to the loading dock, his fellow passengers awake from the brief nap they had enjoyed, gently leaning on each other on the front bench. They have an hour's time to load suits, fins, masks, gloves and all the other necessary paraphernalia into the van to accommodate six tours, completely rigging out five to eight tourists.

Chuck punches in the front door's security code and then rolls up the loading dock gate from the inside. The three of them take the stairs to the office on the second floor. A computer scans their fingerprints and clocks them in for the day. Snatching up the client printout, they return downstairs and enter the storage house.

Kept at a constant thirty degrees Celsius, the room is damp, close and smells of rubber and stale sea water spiced with a touch of sweat. About a hundred sets of diving suits, thermal under suits, gloves and caps hang here to dry for the next day's use. Sam unzips his overall, letting the top half rest on his hips to avoid breaking into a sweat and then freezing when he goes back outside. Icelandic spring temperatures usually hover at around six degrees.

Working in silence, they concentrate on collecting the necessary number of suits in corresponding sizes, taking matching gloves and caps from the drying racks and packing them neatly into transport boxes. They then load the boxes into the van with the rest of the equipment. Sam has a box reserved for chocolate powder and hot water in his hands – it warms up tourists when they come out of Silfra – when Drake comes into the shop's kitchenette.

"Did you know," Sam informs him with a grin, "that no one in Switzerland has ever heard of this instant Swiss chocolate mix?" He finishes up packing.

"I thought I was clear yesterday. You are not allowed to work until they have closed their investigation Your replacements have already been notified. Mikey, Julia and Emma will take your shifts, but they're barely up so I have to go wake them and bring them here since you three took the van." Drake eyed him earnestly.

"Well there you have it," Sam replied, keeping his tone carefully casual. "If we hadn't gotten here on time, the first tour would have been delayed. Besides," he added seriously, "We need something to do! Don't you have anything to keep us occupied while we're waiting? Clean up around here? After what happened, just sitting around twiddling our thumbs is not an option!"

"Agreed. We'll find something for you to do. But first, you have to go the police. You have an appointment at eight and will make your statements then," Drake commands before softening, "I know how you feel, and I'm on your side. I am sure everything will work out. Just be patient."

Chuck and Marie join them. Marie asks quietly, "What do they want to question us about? Are we being accused or suspected of something?"

"Don't worry, it's just routine. Six months ago, a Chinese woman drowned. It was a big deal. But beside tightening safety regulations, nothing happened. As you know, our customers are obligated to sign a liability disclaimer. The authorities just want to be sure that none of you were negligent."

"But I was negligent!" Chuck maintains, smiling sardonically. "I wasn't watching them for moment. I wasn't five meters away, fumbling around with the camera and when I looked up, the good lady had vanished!"

"Listen up and listen good!" Drake plants himself in front of the trio. "By no means will you attest to anything like that! No one can expect us to watch the group every second of the tour. These are not beginners we're talking about! They are all certified divers and have received clear instructions before the tour. The American woman disobeyed strict instructions not to leave the group. She probably wanted to make a spectacular selfie to post on her Facebook page. Even if you had been a meter behind her, the drama would have played out anyway. There was nothing you could have done! So, get a grip on yourselves and do not damage your or our business's reputation. Do you understand?"

Chuck and Marie nod, Chuck curtly, Marie somewhat conscience-stricken. Only Sam is amused. He is well acquainted with the situation. In his corporate guise, complaints were lodged against him every few months or so. In the beginning, he lost sleep and worried himself sick over them, wondering which obscure legal line he had crossed. At some point, he realized it was all part of the game. Just follow the lawyers' advice and the case would eventually sink into the red tape swamp, never to surface again. Until the next time around. That's the way of the business world. Success means taking advantage of every possible loophole and leeway and there will always be someone who objects to how success is attained. Only this time, a person suffered damage to life and limb, that's something holly new to Sam. And he doesn't have a lawyer here to back him up. Still, he is certain that none of them did anything irregular, and certainly not illegal.

"Since Marie wasn't involved in the tour, she doesn't have to go to the police. They may want her statement at a later date, though," Drake explains. As the two men are making for the stairs and their date with the police, Drake calls Sam back.

"It might be that I have something for you. One of our affiliates, Lava Dive, called in. You know, the one offering exclusive VIP tours for the rich and beautiful who are too good to dive with the rabble. They asked for you by name."

"Who could that be?" Sam asks curiously.

Drake winks, "A Brazilian beauty and her fiancé. But let's wait and see how the investigation goes, okay?"

Sam nods and takes the stairs, scanning his memory. Who could that be, he asks himself again? Who even knows he is here in Iceland and working as a diving guide? Of course! He had proudly announced his new job and location on Facebook. Hmmm, he only knows one Brazilian beauty. A few years ago, she was his girlfriend for a while and would have married him in a heartbeat. But he was twenty years her senior and, in the end, he backed out of the relationship. It was a decision that he sometimes still regrets. Still, rich and famous? Bruna is neither, at least she wasn't at the time they separated.

They took off in the second company van, burning rubber. They would have to change out of their diving gear and into shirt and trousers for the interviews. Drake insisted they do so. They couldn't turn up at the police station geared up for a tour. Drake had ensured the authorities that they would not be allowed back in the water until they were absolved.

THREE

They are running late, so instead of circling the side streets for a free parking space they are forced to slip into an exorbitant one on Hlemmur Square. It wouldn't look good if they showed up even a minute later than scheduled for their interviews. Hlemmur Square was once a large marketplace opening directly behind the city gates. Today, it is a bus station running down Laugavegur Street. Laugavegur roughly translates into Wash Way, an old tribute to the path women took regularly to the hot springs where, in earlier days, laundry was carried to be washed. The police station is right around the corner, marking the beginning of Reykjavik's main commercial thoroughfare. They park and run for the doors.

Sam takes deep, calming breaths as they walk down the pearl-grey corridor. Standard issue posters hang on the walls informing visitors of how to safeguard themselves against the varying number of crimes that purportedly hardly ever occur in Iceland. Occasionally a door opens onto the hallway and a civil servant exits with files clamped under his or her arm. They consistently give the two men a friendly nod before vanishing behind another door. Sam and Chuck take seats on the plastic cup chairs lining the walls. A plainclothes officer comes out of a room across the hall, looks at them and without a word of greeting nods to Chuck, who rises and follows the man into the room. The door closes firmly behind them.

After what seems like an eternity, the door opens again releasing a casually smiling Chuck. The officer's hand lies gently on his shoulder, steering him out into the corridor. Chuck gives Sam a nod and meanders toward the exit. He turns around, "I need a smoke. I'll wait for you outside." Sam's eyebrows hit his hairline. Chuck was rippling tension before the interview, despite his attempts at hiding it. Now, here he is, nearly arrogant and decidedly nonchalant. What went on in there? He will soon find out.

The investigator signals to Sam. He rises and follows the man into the questioning room. Sam sits down at the solitary table in the center of the room. The only other items in the otherwise naked space are two chairs, a bottle of water, a glass and a recording device on the table. No shelves, no pictures on the walls. Blinds cover the two windows and only the muffled sounds of traffic on

Laugavegur Street remind you that there's an out there out there.

"Jón Sigurdson," the inspector introduces himself laconically. Son of Sigurd, Sam thinks. When they're young, Icelanders can decide whether to take on their father's or their mother's name. Sigurdson could just as easily have chosen to be Marieson or Friedason. But that's wholly beside the point, get with the program! Chuck's unexpected serenity sent off alarm bells in his head. What's going on here?

"Good morning, sir, my name is Samuel Frei," he absurdly announces, extending his hand, which Sigurdson ignores. Instead, he explains to Sam that the interview will be recorded and anything he says can and will be used against him in a court of law. He smiles briefly. Silence. Sam is equally silent.

"What brings you to our country, Mr. Frei?" Sigurdson finally begins the interview.

Sam hesitates a moment before answering, "I earn my living as a diving guide for Silfra

Scuba. I also want to tour your beautiful country and become acquainted with the people and customs here."

Sigurdson nods and smiles. Again, he falls silent, eying Sam sharply. After a pause, he continues, "We have looked into your record, Mr. Frei. You are, or were, a highly placed manager. It is also on your record in Switzerland that you were once accused of assault and unlawful detention. The case was settled out of court." Sigurdson's voice is calm, almost a whisper, but Sam could clearly hear the disapproving undertone.

Silence. Sam swallows hard. His mouth is dry, and he feels his muscles stiffen, holding him erect in the chair. The investigation is taking an unexpected path he has no desire to travel.

He remembers the C-level rules, laid out for Chief Executive Officers – among whose ranks he until recently counted himself. The only reliable thing that sets a CEO apart from the rest of the rabble is his intuition. He must absorb his counterpart with all senses alert. No one ever tells you exactly what they mean. People apply flattery, purposely omit essentials and adorn their statements. Leadership qualities are not decisive in this line of work. Decisive is the ability to filter information, to gauge one's counterpart, to elicit additional facts and then ultimately assess the situation. Pay no attention to what is said, rather to how it is said. Sam was masterful when it came to letting his counterpart know that he knows exactly what they're playing at and have but this one chance to be taken seriously. Otherwise the meeting is over, and their credibility conclusively destroyed. Over the years of his career, few understood what this rule really implies, but Sam did. And he knows what that means for him now. Sigurdson wants the truth and nothing but.

"That was long ago and has nothing to do with current events leading to this interview," Sam remarks.

"That is not for you to decide," Sigurdson promptly responds.

"Okay, for the record," Sam enunciates slowly and clearly, bending demonstratively toward the microphone and speaking to the table.

"I'm what you might call a dropout, or better a downshifter. I completed my diving instructor training five years ago. I came to Iceland for a change of scenery. I am not dependent on my diving instructor's income, but my colleagues and boss do not know that.

And yes, eight years ago I had a violent argument with my second wife. I thought she was the love of my life, but she was only out for my excellent income. Our marriage lasted all of six months. When I discovered her true motives for marrying me, we had a fight. I slapped her around and locked her in the bedroom, so I could pack my things in peace. I didn't know at the time that there was actually a crime called deprivation of liberty. After paying her a most generous compensation, my ex-wife withdrew the assault complaint and the district attorney dropped all charges. But he maintained I was a beast and therefore insisted on putting a blemish on my record. I have never been sentenced and am certainly not proud of what I did, nor pleased to be reminded of it, sir!"

Sam looks up from the microphone and locks eyes with the heavyset policeman across the table. Sigurdson leans back in his chair, lacing his fingers behind his head.

"Much better," he says to Sam and leans forward, "now maybe we can stop playing around and can get to the real reason you are here – your negligent behavior toward a client entrusted to you. Your prior history reflects an aggressive reaction to stress, leading to a lack of impulse control."

Sam forgets to breathe. What the hell? Do they really believe he is responsible? A lack of impulse control? Bullshit! Did this man maneuver Chuck into incriminating him? Is that why Chuck was so cheerful when he left?

If at all, they had both been negligent, having lost sight of a diver for a second. Even if he was the group leader and primarily responsible, which includes monitoring Chuck to ensure he was also doing his job, it was his impulses that saved them. Of course, he didn't weigh the risks! The situation called for immediate action, so he acted.

Sam looks at Sigurdson's raised eyebrows.

"What's going through your mind, Mr. Frei?" he asks, leaning back again.

"Nothing. The accusation took me completely by surprise. I am not aware of any negligence," Sam replies.

"Then tell me what happened, from the beginning. By the way, the accident victim…," he leaves through his files, "Ah, here it is, Pamela Meyers, is in excellent health and has already made her statement. She declined to lodge a complaint of negligent assault or to file for damages due to pain and suffering. You're a lucky man, Mr. Frei! All the same, it is our job to find out if any misconduct took place and if you should be permitted to keep the professional diving license the Iceland authorities issued in your name. Understood?"

Sigurdson demands, half prone in his seat, waving one foot to an unheard waltz.

Sam nods, and his shoulders slowly sink back to their normal position. That's good news! The last thing he needs is a lawsuit, even if he has the lawyers and funds to defend himself. Battling an American lawyer is no picnic. They do not shy away from holding you liable when your disclaimer fails to mention that diving could cause a broken fingernail, suing for damages of a thousand dollars or more. And winning.

Sam also leans back in his chair and closes his eyes. "Let me tell you what happened. The whole incident keeps replaying in my mind like a horror movie anyway."

"Roll 'em," Sigurdson brusquely commands.

Sam plunges into his memory and begins, "Marie, Chuck and I guided the three Americans through the standard registering procedure. We verified each dry diving license and made sure that the clients read and sign the liability disclaimer, taking full responsibility for themselves. We distributed each item of equipment, helped the clients mount scuba tanks, diving regulators and buoyancy control devices.

Chuck managed the briefing, explaining how they would proceed and clearly stating what not to do, which included that it is absolutely forbidden to dive into caves in the underwater canyon as they lead to unknown depths and were highly precarious, to boot.

I led the diving formation and Chuck brought up the rear, keeping an eye on them all. I guess you know that every customer is required to have certified training in dry diving and must verify diving experience within the last six months before we can allow them in the water.

Marie was our surface support, helping clients get into their gear and enter the canyon. She would be waiting for us after the tour to assist the customers out of the water, out of their suits and escort them safely to the parking lot. Up until this point, everything was going smoothly."

Sam opens his eyes a crack to see if Sigurdson is still listening. He nods encouragingly. Sam releases the pause button, closes his eyes and his mind movie reels forward.

"I checked the buoyancy controls on the couple. He was in his mid-fifties and carried a goodly one hundred and fifty kilos live weight and his girl-friend was no less hefty. I made sure they carried enough lead to compensate for the suits' uplift while allowing them to dive down, but not too much or they would sink like stones. Chuck did the same with the third member of the group, Pamela, a willowy, attractive Asian-American traveling alone and allocated to this tour. I remember Marie rolling her eyes when Chuck suggested I look after the couple while he attends to the almond-eyed Pamela. Once they were outfitted, the middle-aged couple waddled off with me from the parking lot where we distribute the gear. They certainly huffed and puffed beneath the nearly forty kilos of equipment they had added to their generous live weight, but they were making it. They remined me of harp seals. Chuck had to carry both his own gear as well as Pamela's to the entry point as it weighed nearly as much as she did. She would never have covered the one-hundred-meter distance from parking lot to entry point in full re-galia. I could have sworn Marie was peeved be-cause instead of helping Chuck lug the equip-ment, she turned and went off to wait at the entry point. I have no idea if they've got something go-ing or not. But Chuck, macho man that he is, didn't ask for help, either. He merely shouldered the gear and trudged on, bringing up the rear. By the time he got to the entry point, he was rather red in the face.

After re-checking all aspects of the clients' equipment, we dove down to a depth of ten meters where the tour would begin. The first leg was approximately one hundred meters, leading over a flat plateau to the second leg.

We were lucky. The lighting was indescribable that day and the canyon more than lived up to its nickname, Silver Lady. Countless shimmering tones of silvery greys and blues. The sun broke through the clouds and flooded the canyon in staggering white light. The water temperature was two degrees Celsius, and so incredibly pure it was if diving into clean, clear, fluid glass. The one-hundred-meter underwater visibility here never ceases to move me. There's nowhere else in the Earth's endless oceans like that.

Chuck and I took the obligatory photos of our clients against a backdrop of craggy, sharply vertical canyon walls, including, of course, a shot of each tourist at the canyon's most narrow passage. Here, with outstretched arms, they are sandwiched between the two continents, touching one with each hand. Easy-going all the way. The divers were quite competent and obviously not newcomers to ice-cold water nor to diving in unwieldy dry suits. There was no uncontrolled surfacing, no reeling when adjusting their suits, no clumsy contact with the rocky walls. Excellent.

I was satisfied and relaxed a bit, stopped turning around every five meters to check the group. After all, Chuck was watching from behind.

And then I heard the alarm, metal banging on a dip tank, so I bent down and looked between my legs. Chuck was tapping his camera on his tank. When he saw he had my attention, he pointed to a cave opening. I turned to where the two tubby clients were floating nearby like harp seals, but Pamela was nowhere to be seen. My alarm bells went off immediately and I took a look at the surface. The water was so clear, I would have to see her, even if she had gone further away. And if she were behind a rock or crag, I would see her air bubbles. Shit! I signaled the couple to wait where they were and was with Chuck in two strokes. He pointed to a cave plunging steeply downward at a sharp angle. I pointed two fingers first at Chuck, then at his eyes and back to the couple. I pointed to myself and the cave opening.

Chuck wagged his finger in my face. We all know how extremely precarious the caves can be since daily tremors cause shifting, new cracks and suchlike. Touch just one, delicately placed loose stone and you can trigger an avalanche, burying anyone foolhardy enough to go inside. I couldn't just leave her there; it just wasn't an option. I was in charge and felt responsible for the group. I had to get her out to safety.

I looked into the cave's opening. Directly behind the entrance, the cave took a steep turn downwards and seconds after I entered, it was pitch black. I switched on my lamp. Swirling sediment limited my visibility, but when I looked up, I saw her. Thank goodness! I am both relieved and angry at her for not following safety instructions. Then I see air bubbles boiling around her. She's twisting and turning, frantically seeking an exit in the narrow channels leading upwards and allowing narrow strips of light to penetrate the cave. I knew if she saw me, she would grab hold of me and not let go. In such tight quarters, that would be the end of us both.

I turned off my lamp and rose up behind her, catching hold of her tank. I intended to pull her down and backward to the cave's opening. It was only a few meters away. She was so surprised at first that she did not resist. But then she realized I was pulling her away from where she believed the exit to be. She panicked. I turned the woman around, so we were mask to mask and in the pallid light, I saw her bulging eyes and knew it was too late to try to reason with her. Her senses were locked behind a bastion of neurons firing adrenaline full force. Her brain was fueled with pure instinct, the fight or flight impulse blocked all rational thought. Unable to flee, she fought me. She ripped my mask from my face. She tore at my air tubes. Afraid of losing my source of oxygen, I clamped my teeth down on the mouthpiece and thrust her away. Still, I kept my left hand on her tank and dove beneath her. It was a nightmare."

Sitting bolt upright in his chair, Sam is back in the cave. Behind his closed eyes, Pamela is clinging to him and fighting him at the same time. Sigurdson, his eyes still fixed on the ceiling, is listening intently.

"With my free hand I started pulling both of us backward toward the exit, groping for secure cracks in the rock wall for leverage. All I wanted was to get out of there. The rocks wobbled like loose teeth in an old man's mouth, but they held fast. Without a mask, my vision is very blurred, the light shimmering at the cave's mouth my beacon. The few meters seemed like miles and miles. I am having trouble breathing. Pamela is trying to twist out of my grip, but she can't get her hands behind the tank. I remember repeating to myself the mantra drilled into us a million times during training: Inhale, you can doooo it; exhale, you knoooow how.

A meter or two before we reach the opening, we stopped dead. Something was caught in the rocky chaos. Pamela's GoPro camera, clipped to her hand, was stuck in a crack. She was writhing and pulling at it with all her strength. I caught hold of the band with my right hand, scraping my left on the cave ceiling as her tank rose. I ripped off the camera and freed her arm, using the strength of mortal fear. I was close to panicking now myself and Pamela was kicking wildly with her flippers, banging her tank on the ceiling and reaching for my arm. She wrenched loose the ring system attaching my gloves to the rest of the suit. Within seconds, icy water flooded my suit from toe to chest, I was shocked into calm. I knew damn well that I had only two minutes before losing consciousness.

That's when my mind took over. Mechanically, I pulled hard on Pamela's legs to get her out of the cave. Her head struck the ceiling and like a music box ballerina winding down, all movement stopped. She hung limp in the water.

I took the last meter and saw the saving surface above us. I pulled the American in a tight embrace and pressed my knees into her underbelly with all my remaining strength to empty her lungs. A rapid rise from ten meters' depth would expand the air in her lungs to twice its volume. In Pamela's un-conscious condition they would burst like two bal-loons. I could vaguely see bubbles stream from her mouth and pushed the inflator button on her buoyancy vest. Everything I have learned about diving; its dangers and rescue procedures is en-grained in my mind. And although my body was quickly surrendering to the inevitable, I could carry out the necessary motions automatically. For a few seconds, we floated in silence until the vest's enor-mous propulsion rocketed us to the surface. In a vortex of bubbles, we shot almost completely out of the water. I spit my mouthpiece out and hun-grily swallowed fresh air, and for a moment the spots before my eyes vanished. I pushed the air button on my suit, hoping the inflation would at least protect my chest but it only pressed the wa-ter up and over my shoulders. The cold clung to me like icy wet pajamas. I had to get out of the water or die trying.

I inflated my vest and attempted to reanimate Pamela, but I could only muster a weak puff. I remember thinking, this is it. Images of my childhood arose, and there's me laughing and racing around on a merry-go-round. And then it went very quiet, I could only hear the whistling of my breath. The cold had vanished, and I was endlessly tired."

Sam collapses in his seat, reliving the leaden exhaustion he is describing. In the meantime, Sigurdson has his chin on his laced fingers, gazing at Sam as if watching an action thriller. Sam was oblivious, his mind and heart completely absorbed in the events indelibly printed onto his body.

"Then I caught sight of Chuck shooting up next to me, followed by the two harp seals. I dimly heard Chuck blasting his whistle, sending an SOS to any other divers in the area and thought I saw him catch hold of Pamela and start swimming over to the lagoon. It's only fifty meters. I somehow got on my back and paddled as well as I could to the exit point. It seemed like miles and then guides from varying groups surrounded me, their flippers making suds of the calm water.

I sensed the couple behind me, but they were on their own.

Hands took hold of me and turned me on my back. My legs no longer existed, my hands and arms felt clamped in vises and there was an iceberg on my chest. Breathing had become nearly impossible. I looked up into the white sky, saw shredded clouds pass over and surrendered to the space-less, timeless white shroud as it settled over me.

The next thing I became aware of was someone hammering my chest and shouting my name. Several pairs of hands zipped, unclicked and wrestled me out of my no-longer-dry suit. I tried to resist but my body didn't respond, I no longer even seemed to have a body. My perception of myself, of life at all, was a small knot of diffuse thoughts swimming in a dislocated head, somewhere connected to a tiny circle of chesty flesh. Like a dying dolphin, they rolled me in a blanket, picked me up and ran. At the van they unwrapped me and I heard Chuck bellowing, "Only on his chest, only on his chest! Nothing warm on the extremities! When blood starts flowing through his frozen arms and legs, he'll die of shock when it reaches his heart!"

They laid towels drenched in the hot water meant for post-tour hot chocolate on my chest. The pain was excruciating, and I blacked out once or twice for a few seconds. But the pain also brought me back to consciousness. It felt like an obese fakir was sitting on his bed of nails on my chest – with the nail side down. Each breath was a pair of pliers tearing and pulling the skin down over my ribcage. I could only breathe in fits and starts. I could feel my heart beating hard and slowly against my throat, speeding up, getting louder, a crescendo. The sound reminded me of a lawnmower starting up in the middle of winter – sputter, spit, die, sputter, choke, rev. And then I started shaking. Merciless electroshocks. I literally bounced across the floor of the van, flailing from one corner to the next. An internal earthquake that went on and on and on. I couldn't speak, I wished I could scream or lose consciousness, the pain was that powerful. Eventually, I managed to stammer, "A…A…Amee…riri…caannnn." Chuck stroked my face, "Yes, dammit! She is alive, thanks to you, you damned crazy Swiss and she's in much better shape than you are!! She's got a fine bump on the head and is in a mild state of shock – the stupid bitch! She nearly got you both killed!"

A half an hour later, I was sitting at the packing table, wrapped tightly in a blanket, hot chocolate in my trembling hands, watching a medical team load Pamela, a lovely, stupid American into the helicopter and fly off. In the ensuing silence, it dawned on me what had just happened, and how incredibly lucky I had been. I was furious, proud, grateful and shocked. Every ten seconds I was flooded with another emotion; felt as if there was one of those ancient dive bells between me and the rest of the world; I wanted to scream, laugh and cry all at once while I sat on that table and tried to gather my wits.

The doctor had examined my circulation several times before lifting off, extracting the promise that I would go to the clinic for a thorough checkup once back in Reykjavik.

The harp seals were once again in their street clothes and sat down next to me. I listened patiently to their songs of praise, their verbal medals for heroism, bore their repeated pats on the back and selfies with me in the middle and was utterly relieved when they finally, after shaking my shaking hand repeatedly, went on their way. Clutching Chuck in tight hugs, they said goodbye to him, too, pressing a hundred-dollar bill into his hand. When they were gone, Chuck waved the money like a victory banner as he rejoined Marie and me. All gratuities are shared equally with the team.

Marie hugged me close, sharing her warmth, and rubbed my shoulders vigorously to help stop the quaking. "That's just my nerves," I said, teeth chattering. "I feel like a codfish on deck." Marie planted a kiss on my forehead and a thrill of excitement proved there was still life in this old boy. Chuck dangled Pamela's GoPro on his fingers. The guides had found it. "This could be important evidence! You know how quick Americans are to call their lawyers. This will prove what happened," he said impishly. Then he helped me to my feet, and we drove to the clinic.

Sam opens his eyes. His heart is racing, and goosebumps prickle from his crown to his fingertips. Reliving the drama has exhausted him and he gratefully accepts the glass of water Sigurdson offers. He has recounted the tale exactly as it occurred, uncensored, unfiltered, without a thought to how it may be received. He gazes impassively into Sigurdson's eyes.

"Congratulations," Sigurdson says after a moment. "Your statement concurs with your colleague's and with Pamela Meyers'."

"And what does that mean?" Sam asks, puzzled.

"That I can close the case and you're free to go. I didn't expect anything else, really." Sigurdson rises lightly from his seat, his diffident Viking visage reveals nothing of what is going on behind his eyes.

"A bit of advice: Come directly to us next time instead of waiting for an invitation. Or even better, don't let there be a next time," he adds with the ghost of a smile, steering Sam to the door, his hand on Sam's shoulder.

In the corridor, Sam nods wordlessly, once more offering Sigurdson his hand. This time, the man takes it.

Outside, Chuck is waiting impatiently and when he sees Sam, runs up and clasps him in bear hug, offering a burning cigarette from which Sam draws deeply. "It went well," Sam says in response to the question in Chuck's eyes. "It looks like we're free and clear."

"Yesss!" Chuck agrees, throwing his fist in the air. "What else did you expect?"

Chuck drives Sam to the clinic again since without a second thorough checkup Drake will certainly not let him back in the water. Delayed hypothermia symptoms can hit the system over twenty-four hours later. Sam allows himself to be probed and prodded. No negative findings. The doctor recommends a few days of rest all the same. He should not underestimate the enormous strain hypothermia had put on his heart, particularly at his age. Relieved, Sam strolls back to the parking lot where Chuck is waiting for him.

"Let's go, old man!" Chuck teases him when he gets in the van.

Sam punches him lightly in the shoulder. "Call me old man again and I'll show you just how old I am!"

"No need, I saw you in action. You might be old enough to be my father, but mine couldn't manage five steps in full gear. If we had been depending on him, we'd be preparing his funeral right now, and that woman's, too! I salute you!"

High on relief, they breeze through the city and head for Domino, the pizza parlor not far from V18. This is a moment to celebrate.

Just as he licks his fingers clean of the greasy calzone he had wolfed down, chasing it with a coke, Sam's cellphone rings. He gets up from the curb where they are holding their feast, stretches in the sun and takes the call. The cardboard calzone box lays abandoned on the street, and Sam, listening intently, casually picks it up and tosses it in the trashcan. He has yet to speak a word to whoever's talking.

"Okay, I'll be there in fifteen minutes," and cuts the call. When he looks up at Chuck, he's smiling from ear to ear. "I have a tour for Lava Dive this afternoon. Some pretty Brazilian girl wants me and no one else to guide her and her fiancé on a snorkeling tour in Silfra."

"You lucky bastard!" Chuck groans, his mouth full of pizza and swiping windblown hairs from his face.

"Let's go, we're back in business!" Sam waves the keys happily.

Chuck quickly finishes up his meal and joins Sam. Arms over each other's shoulders, they do an improvised sirtaki, hopping and laughing on the way to the van. Seagulls watch from above, shrieking their comments while the lunch crowd inside the pizzeria point, grin and embellish rumors about the day's Silfra heroes with gossip of their own.

FOUR

Sam slides the helicopter door shut with a loud bang and slips on the headphones hanging in front of him. He can hear Bruna and Pedro kissing and cooing over the intercom. Demonstratively clearing his throat, he announced, "Enjoy the ride! Iceland is so beautiful, you'll be amazed. The wind blows hard and constant here, so our copter might dance around a bit, but there's no need to worry." He hopes they get the underlying message: the mics are on and everyone in the cabin can hear you, no matter what kind of sounds you make. The pilot grins and rolls his eyes as he eases the Jet Ranger into the wind, lifting off from Isavia, the inland airport and quickly rising to a secure elevation. As Sam predicted, the machine waltzes alarmingly before gaining velocity to fly over the city, its course set for Þingvellir National park.

***

Sam drove directly to Lava Dive's noble offices after dropping Chuck off at V18. Drake has arranged for Ian to partner with Sam. He will be waiting for them with the equipment van at Silfra. The helicopter is due in fifteen minutes and Sam wants a moment to meet and greet his two clients, especially if it really is Bruna.

It is. Bruna and a young man he's never seen before are lounging in the luxurious leather easy chairs, conversing comfortably while they wait for him. It's obvious that they share a deep connection that still bears the freshness of a relatively new relationship.

Sam experiences a distinct moment of discomfort. He is assaulted by memories of passionate tropical nights in Rio; of sweat slick skin on sweat slick skin; of remote hotels to which they had escaped on weekends and enjoyed a wealth of good wine and excellent conversation; hiatuses of languid, philosophical reflection before their hunger for one another revivified. Bruna is intelligent, has studied genetics and can speak five languages fluently. She was genuinely in love with Sam and not after a Swiss passport. She loved him, wanted to introduce him to her family, to marry him. Sam was deeply flattered. He thoroughly enjoyed her intelligence, her stunning body and her youth. He was so proud to stroll along the beaches with such a beautiful, charming, twenty-years-younger lover.

Still, he could not help imagining what it would be like when he was seventy and she only fifty. He simply did not have the courage to surrender to love. Surely he will lose her in time. Bruna was devastated. Sam tirelessly encouraged her to find a man more suited to her, closer to her age. This was no comfort whatsoever and only sparked her anger. She explained again and again that their age difference meant nothing and never would. She had never wanted children, even before she met him, and that was not going to change. But Sam remembered how he viewed the world at thirty and knew that this could, and most likely would, change. Still, in the final account, his decision was driven by bald fear. Fear of making promises he might not be able to keep. Fear of abandonment and, ultimately, fear of the genuine love and respect he felt for Bruna. He didn't believe he could live up to her and his old, basic conviction that he was a dreadful phony held him in its iron grip. He didn't trust himself. He'd tried marriage and failed, twice. And in addition to the financial debacles his divorces had triggered, they had also flattened him emotionally. So now, the prospect of failing again led him to hide behind their age difference, played the selfless one who only wanted the woman he loved to find someone better, someone younger. He was a coward.

A few months after their breakup, he regretted his decision and tried to approach Bruna again. She refused his calls. He had not heard anything from her for four years and now she was here, with her fiancé.

Bruna still has her slim figure, bordering on reedy and if it wasn't for her artificially enlarged breasts, her shape would be androgynous. She is wearing a green overall zipped down just enough to proudly display her generous bosom.

She greets Sam enthusiastically, jumping from her seat, pulling him close and kissing him gently on the mouth. Sam keeps his hands firmly in his pockets. He is deeply discomfited and throws glances over to her fiancé. Still caught in her embrace, Bruna's hazelnut eyes gaze at him until he answers the look. Is there still a touch of melancholy in her eyes? he asks himself. At that moment she releases him and goes to her fiancé, kissing him passionately as if in answer to his question. She leads the man to Sam.

"Let me introduce Pedro, my darling fiancé," she says with a smile, placing a hand on either shoulder as they shake hands. Sam feels like a schoolboy whose teacher demands he make up with another boy after they had been fighting. He dries his sweaty hands on his pants and swallows several times.

"Parabens! Congratulations! Tudo bem?" The Brazilian pleasantries stick in Sam's throat, but he forces them out, shaking hands and giving Pedro a hug, as Brazilians always do. No haphephobia there! An abraço, an embrace, expresses solidarity and friendship. The two men take seats while Bruna goes to the ladies room.

"Bruna has told me all about the two of you. You are a wise man, Sam, wise and strong. I can imagine it was not easy for you to let Bruna go, but I am profoundly grateful that you did," Pedro confides while his bride-to-be is away.

Bruna returns, waving her hands and Sam grins discreetly. She still needs to disinfect her hands several times a day.

The helicopter is delayed, and the secretary is still waiting for confirmation from Ian that their equipment and light meal has arrived at Silfra in Þingvellir Park.

The trio make themselves comfortable in the opulent seats and Sam learns that Pedro is actually Pedro IV, a direct descendent of Pedro II who was crowned Emperor of Brazil in 1840. As the country progressed and became the leading export of caoutchouc, the now former royal family earned immeasurable wealth, which they carefully guarded throughout the years of military reign and the ensuing democracy. Sam is impressed. He didn't even know that Brazil had once been a monarchy.

Bruna colors with passion as she describes to Sam how they, after the wedding, plan to invest a greater part of the family fortune in Brazil's rampant poverty and in the massive gaps in the education system. Pedro maintains that those who have received more than enough from life are obligated to give something in return. He sketches out a number of projects they have launched in Rio's countless favelas.

Sam listens attentively, nodding his agreement, until his mind begins to wander. Pedro is an inspiration. How much is enough? When is someone content and when does giving turn into asceticism or even self-denial? He assumes the two of them will give as long as it doesn't infringe on their luxurious lifestyle. But anyway! He could share his wealth, too, couldn't he? Maybe not as generously, but certainly enough for small, good deeds? When exactly is enough enough? When is it not enough? Is there a limit? A definition?

He is reminded of a keynote speaker at a congress he attended. The man had flown to the event in his private jet yet spoken eloquently about the world's poverty and the need for action. At the banquet following the congress, Sam had asked the man to explain this paradox. Why hadn't he taken a first-class flight? It would have been nearly as luxurious, and the cost difference would have been enough to give thousands of cataract-stricken Africans their sight again. The prominent business guru gave him a sly wink and said he needed the jet for his image. If he didn't indulge himself people would not take him seriously. So, it goes to follow, Sam muses, that enough is not only material wealth, it is also a matter of status. Is humanity irrevocably programmed to reach for more and more and more? Are we doomed to hunt and gather because of some stone age instinct? Can this be why there is no clear definition of enough? Is having more than enough an inherent need to ensure survival or does it serve to quash competitors in the fight for superior genes? Is wealth and power driven by a desperate need to control other people? Are we so insecure about our place in the world that we can only justify our existence by erecting a fortress of riches?

And what about Pedro and Bruna? Isn't their blatant altruism just another form of attention-grabbing? Of being publicly noble? He admits, it would still do a lot of people good. Maybe it is best to take a pragmatic view, like foregoing the private jet and taking a first-class flight. At least then, their shamelessly expensive Silfra tour would provide Lava Dive's two employees a good income.

Bruna seems to guess what Sam is thinking. He knows so well how she loves a good philosophical discourse on ethics. Her eyes bright, she draws breath to speak. At that moment, a gust of wind makes them turn to the open door. Their pilot has arrived. He flips up his visor, claps his gloved hands and announces, "We're ready! Let's go!"

***

The Jet Ranger glides over Reykjavik's indomitable Hallgrímskirkja, Iceland's imposing Lutheran cathedral, and heads for the harbor. The basin is dotted with typical, burly Icelandic fishing boats and the coast guard fleet. As they thwack over the bay, Sam turns and asks Bruna and Pedro if they want to hear some interesting facts about Iceland. They answered with a simultaneous thumbs up.

"Well," he begins the speech all guides are encouraged to memorize so they can entertain their customers before or after their tours. "The name Reykjavik is Icelandic for smoking bay, which is

attributed to Ingólfur Arnarson and the first settlers when they mistakenly believed the steam rising from the thermal springs was smoke. The city
is the oldest permanent settlement in the country,
dating back to 870. But the population grew so
slowly, it wasn't until 1786 that Reykjavik earned
city status. Today, sixty percent of the three hundred thousand Icelanders live there.

Iceland's land mass lies directly on the Mid-Atlantic Ridge that separates the North American
and European tectonic plates. The ridge runs
along the ocean floor, stretching nearly from pole
to pole, but can only be seen in Iceland. Each
year, the tectonic plates move approximately two
centimeters apart, about the same rate at which
our fingernails grow. This movement explains Iceland's one hundred and eighty active volcanos
and up to six hundred earthquakes a week, most
of which are barely perceptible. But the volcanos
require constant vigilance, posing an uninter-
rupted threat to the population. Over the years,
Iceland has developed a sophisticated, blanket
measuring system to give its inhabitants fair warning of a coming eruption.

We cannot even begin to imagine the hard-
ships endured by Iceland's first pioneers. Even
though, thanks to the Gulf Stream, the climate is

milder than in Canada and a Reykjavik winter is not as cold as winter in New York, still, nothing grows here, making life difficult for both man and beast. Their only wealth was the fishing grounds, and that is what kept them alive. All the same, recurring famine and epidemics brought those hardy people to the edge of obsolescence time and time again. Iceland's population grew very slowly, and it was not until after World War II that prosperity, attained through technology, settled here at last. Today, Iceland is a wealthy land with one of the highest life expectancies worldwide."

At that moment, the eighty square kilometers of Lake Þingvallavatn appear on the horizon. Sam is rendered speechless by its beauty. He has never seen it from the air before and the vision is overwhelming! The lake lies in Þingvellir Ditch surrounded by steep slopes rising to an active volcanic system. Prestahnúkur and Hrafnabjörg rise in the northeast, while in the southwest Hrómundartindur resides. In the center of deepest blue water glittering in the sun, is Sandey, a conical island birthed by the Hengill volcano.

About, fifty kilometers behind the lake you can see Langjökull, the second largest glacier in Iceland. Covering nine hundred and fifty square kilometers, it's about the same size as Dallas, Texas.

Climate change is melting the glacier like butter in the sun, but it is still a solid wall six hundred meters thick, enclosing at least two active volcano systems.

"In terms of the Earth's history, Iceland is very young, not even ten thousand years old," Sam continued. "You get the feeling you can watch the Earth emerging. Look at the moss and lichen-covered lava boulders around the lake. This green shimmering tundra will one day, in about a hundred years, become humus for larger plant life. Those pale purple areas are flowering lupine. Lupine is not indigenous to Iceland. It was imported and planted to help curb unceasing erosion. Now they have spread like weeds all over the country. There you can see groups of pine trees that were planted just a few years ago. They are the only trees that can dig into the meager soil. Before people came, Iceland was almost completely covered in forest and shrubs, but settlers used every stick of wood for their building and heating material needs. Twenty years ago, reforestation began, but it's a slow process."

Here, Sam ends his lecture and watches wild geese rise from the islet in the middle of the lake and flee from the thwocking rotors. They're almost there. Although Sam is accustomed to the mountains and lush valleys of his homeland, Iceland's primeval power and majesty move him on a deeper, more profound level. His clients in the back are equally speechless, the intercom is silent. All of them gaze out the windows, enthralled as the pilot lowers his machine, making a broad, sweeping curve over the lake heading for the landing point nearby Silfra.

The only vehicle on the parking lot that doubles as entry point for snorkel and diving tours, is the Lava Dive van. By this time, six pm, all other tours have ended, and the tourists are snugly back in their hotels. But the sun is still high in the sky. It is a beautiful day.

Sam, Pedro and Bruna follow the footpath from the landing point to the parking lot. The pilot lifts off immediately, pirouetting his adieu. A private car will come to collect the couple and take them back to their hotel.

As they approach, Ian comes around the van. His arms wide open, he greets them in a resonant bass, "Welcome to the most beautiful place on Earth!" And proceeds to shake hands with Bruna and Pedro.

"You're a living, breathing Viking," Bruna claims, impressed by Ian's broad back, bright red mane and full beard.

"Not exactly, milady. I'm a born and bred English-man, but there's plenty of Norse blood running through my veins," he informs her with a smile. "Now let's get to it. I will brief you on everything you need to know for your snorkeling adventure between the continents while our boy here prepares the gear. Are you ready? Can we get started? Oh, and before I forget, the toilets are over there, and I highly recommend you go before you get into your suits. Afterwards, it gets awkward," Ian explains, his eyes full of impish amusement.

Sam grins, shaking his head. Apparently, he's the boy, so he makes for the van while Bruna and Pedro turn expectantly to Ian who hops lightly onto a packing table and picks up the tin plate depicting Silfra. As if on cue, a slew of ducks waddles up to them quacking melodiously. Like buskers, they humbly insist on their share of attention and chocolate cookies. Rarely are they disappointed.

As instructed, Pedro and Bruna fold their clothes and place them in the waterproof boxes and don padded overalls. Bruna struts her stuff, calling to Pedro, "Look, cara mia, I finally have a lovely, broad Mulatta butt!"

Sam takes photos from every angle and of each new step in preparations. While he is leading the twosome into Silfra, Ian will take over as cameraman, making sure the family album, social media and posterity have their due. At two thousand dollars a tour, this is but one of the services included.

Ian begins briefing his clients, "I'll first give you some information on Silfra, then we'll talk about snorkeling here. So, here we are in Þingvellir National park, the heart of Icelandic culture. It is also a UNESCO World Heritage site. From the tenth to thirteenth centuries, clan chieftains met here to develop, discuss and pass laws governing all of Iceland. Although only a few could vote and participate, the entire population was welcome to watch and listen. The assembly also served as a kind of Supreme Court. During the gatherings, weddings took place, land was allocated, and disputes were settled. There was also the occasional execution. Men were pushed from the top of the waterfall over there and women were simply thrown into Silfra.

The Icelanders' boast that they created the first democratic government is not an empty one. Life was extremely hard and cooperation a matter of survival. Feuding was a luxury early Icelanders could not afford."

Ian falls silent for a moment, enjoying the theatrical buildup up to the next part of his talk. He continues, "Iceland rests on the Mid-Atlantic Ridge, a fault dividing the continental plates and running almost clearly from the North to the South pole. There, on the left you can see the beginning of Europe and on our right, is the wall marking North America. A wall, by the way, Donald Trump did not build," he added with a wicked grin. This joke did not always sit well with U.S. Americans, but Pedro and Bruna smiled, obviously amused.

"Silfra is a kind of canyon emerging from a lava field between the plates. It is fed by Langjökull meltwaters which take about fifty years to seep from the glacier to Silfra, maintaining a steady two degrees Celsius regardless of season. You will be more floating than swimming, as seepage is exceptionally slow, making for a languid current. At the end of the tour, however, you should follow Sam into the lagoon, we do not want to call the helicopter back on a rescue mission. Which brings us to the reason you're here, namely snorkeling." Ian pauses to give them the opportunity to ask question, but Pedro and Bruna merely look at him expectantly.

"In a few moments, Sam will help you into your dry diving suits, which are rather bulky and have a very rough surface. Even if you wanted to, you couldn't dive in a dry suit without extra weight. We check and double check the silicon closures on your neck and arms to ensure no water can penetrate the suit. But your hands and head will get wet since the neoprene gloves and caps are not waterproof. This water will create a thin film which actually helps to keep you warm, so don't move your head around or paddle too wildly or fresh water will enter, and you will become very cold very fast. Of course, the areas of your face above and below the mask will get wet. Your lips will become numb within seconds and later you'll look like Angelina Jolie, but only for few minutes."

Ian explains the flippers, gloves and caps, and outlines the tour agenda. He then leads the couple to Sam at the material tables, Sam gives each of them a dry diving suit made of seven-millimeter-thick neoprene. The boots are integrated, and the neck and wrists have tightly fitting silicon cuffs to avoid leakage. The suit is donned through a watertight zipper running across the shoulder. Putting on this suit for the first time makes you feel like the Michelin Man with a noose around his neck, which is exactly how Bruna and Pedro feel right now.

"Try to relax," Sam encourages them when he sees their concerned faces. "It will be better once we're in the water." He gives each of them a pair of gloves, flippers, a mask and snorkel. The caps tend to exacerbate a newbie's discomfort since they fit so tightly and leave only a small oval free, increasing the feeling of breathlessness. Therefore, Sam carries the caps and will put them on them directly before they enter Silfra.

It is a hilarious short march to the stairs leading into Silfra. Pedro and Bruna, waddling like a pair of penguins holding eggs between their webbed feet, could not stop giggling. Sam can detect the hint of hysteria common to inexperienced divers and falls into a relaxed attentiveness. At the stairs, there's a final pulling and tugging on arms and heads until the two are fully attired and their adventure begins.

Sam is the first to enter the water. One after the other, Ian escorts Bruna and Pedro down the steps and into the water, holding onto their hands so they don't slip. Bruna wades in up to her hips and lets herself fall onto her belly. Sam hears her startled "Oh shit!" she wheels her arms and tries to get back on her feet. Sam grasps her arms and sets her upright and she immediately tears her mask from her head.

"You're fine, you're fine. Go slowly now, take your time. Your mind might be shouting life threatening, but it's not and eventually you'll get used to the temperature and your thoughts will calm down," he speaks soothingly and, still holding onto her, waves Pedro over. "Now you try putting your head underwater," Sam instructs him. Pedro does as asked and instantly comes back up, his eyes wide and gasping for breath.

Sam has them sit on the bottom step and practice putting their faces in the water. After a while, their defensively raised shoulders sink, their clenched fists open and their arms stretch out and lay on the water's surface. Now they're ready.

Slowly, Sam pulls them by the hands into the canyon. The water is so incredibly clear and Silfra shimmers in blue grays below. Wildly craggy and fissured, the abyss is both ominous and magical. Gradually, Pedro and Bruno relax and float on the mild current. Sam sees them begin to look around, pointing out various unique formations to one another. Soft as baby's hair, brilliant green alga grows on boulder surfaces posing an electrifying contrast to blues and grays. Feeding solely on sunlight, alga is Silfra's only resident life form, receiving numerous overnight guests as small glittering fish swim up from the lake each evening and dart into countless cave entrances seeking shelter from predators.

They have reached the shallows where the water is only half a meter deep. Sam carefully takes their hands, to avoid them standing upright or banging their legs against precarious rocks. On their left, they see the narrow passage into the lagoon, where the tour will end.

"Look over here, can you see the metal ladder on the other side? That's one hundred meters. Nowhere else in the world will you have such far-reaching underwater visibility," Sam explains. The couple nods, humbled, and Sam notices Bruna stretching her thickly gloved fingers out of the water. They have been in fifteen minutes and she apparently already has painfully cold fingers. Ten more minutes and she'll begin to shake uncontrollably. The suits keep you dry, but the cold still creeps through the neoprene and padded overall. He knew what she was feeling but was accustomed to the cold. It was a certain mindset, like ignoring steady pain, breathing calmly and acknowledging its existence without reacting to it.

Shortly before they reach Silfra's deepest and widest area, the cathedral, Bruna begins to flap her arms again. Her slim body is subcooled. Sam is with her in a heartbeat, turns her over on her back and removes the snorkel from her mouth, "Just relax and float, breath slowly and deeply, I'm going to pull you a bit." She nods with tightly sealed, trembling lips and gazes up in the sky. Pedro appears to be doing fine, giving a thumbs up when Sam asks.

The cathedral is a place of astonishing beauty. It is very like a dream where you find yourself floating just below vaulted ceilings of an enormous church looking down on the nave. Instead of pews, rocks and boulders line the floor and the stained-glass windows are delicate, lacy curtains of alga hanging over the walls. The vision leaves no human being untouched. To have the honor of looking inside Mother Earth, into her wondrous depths, knowing that not far below, magma boils.

Pedro glides gracefully around the boulders and into the lagoon while Sam guides Bruna through to safety. It is a tricky spot as the canyon floor rises to meet the lagoon, causing an increase in the current's strength and velocity. A nearly instant change within one meter's distance. Sam had seen guides have difficulty reaching the lagoon. Gently paddling, Pedro enjoys the lagoon while Sam releases Bruna. She rolls back onto her stomach, not wanting to miss the rare beauty Nature offers. She would not have been surprised when elves and fairies floated out from behind the alga curtains. Sam remains by her side; he notes her quivering head and stilted leg movements. The onset of hypothermia. Side by side, they swim to the steps where Ian is waiting for them.

A few minutes later and they are standing on the steps and Ian collects flippers, masks and caps. He pulls off Bruna's gloves and encloses her frozen hands with his warm ones.

"Que linda!" Pedro laughs gleefully, pointing at Bruna's lips. Ian's promise held true. Bruna attempts a smile but can only turn up the corners of her mouth. Her teeth are chattering uncontrollably. If their walk to the entry reminded of penguins, the walk back to the parking lot resembles storks, only much less elegant. Ian had set up a table with delicate snacks, hot chocolate and tea, but first there are several moments dedicated to tearing, jerking and peeling out of their gear until they sit on the benches, wrapped in soft blankets. Sipping hot chocolate, they click through the photographs on the camera's display. Sam had routinely taken photos of the most spectacular views.

Not much later, a Land Rover pulls in to take them back to the Hilton. The driver invitingly opens the back door, emitting warm, dry air. He has turned the heating up full blast for his still shivering passengers.

"Thank you, it was wonderful," Bruna whispers in Sam's ear as she hugs him goodbye.

"I know, Silfra is a breathtaking lady," Sam grins.

"That's not what I meant. You hurt me so badly, I hated you then. But you were right. I have found an amazing, young man who is perfect for me. I am so grateful! And I'm glad you seem to have finally come home to your natural habitat." And she once more kisses him fleetingly on the lips.

Pedro also hugs him heartily and the two men exchange pats on the back. He invites Sam to a midnight dinner, but he politely refuses. Maybe he'll come for dessert.

"Will we see you again?" Bruna calls from the car door. Sam gives her a thumbs up and the heavy vehicle zips from the parking lot onto Kies Street, heading toward Reykjavik.

"You fool! You let that beauty get away?" Ian chuckles, as the two of them pack the transport boxes.

"Hmmm," Sam grunts without further comment. They scarf down the remaining tasty tidbits and wipe the crumbs from the table which are eagerly snapped up by impatiently fidgeting ducks.

Sam gazes sightlessly out the window as Ian drives over the deserted street that takes them from the elevated plateau through a valley to the Bay of Reykjavik. A couple of grazing Iceland ponies turn their sturdy hindquarters to the wind, indifferently enduring the sudden graupel shower sweeping over the valley.

Soon, the sun will break through the clouds again and life will go on, as it has for Sam since yesterday's horrors. Is Bruna right? Has he found his natural habitat? His former life in stuffy offices and tedious meetings seems to belong to another man altogether.

His inner whirlwind has calmed. He feels at home in his skin despite the frequently foul weather that somehow, too, soothes his restlessness. Iceland has apparently penetrated his fortresses, leading him to his guileless core, deeply embedded in primeval Nature. A mere twenty million years old, Sam responds to the ancient wisdom radiating from the massive mountains, volcanos and lava fields. Or is it the silent, unseen presence of trolls and elves that lend the land its mystical aura, as so many Icelanders still believe? Before building roads and houses, the wee inhabitants of certain lava boulders are respectfully asked if they would kindly to relocate. Should they refuse, it's quite likely construction plans will be scratched or carried out so carefully that the native spirits are not disturbed. Perhaps some find this quaint and laughable, but it is living proof that the human beings honor and cherish their environment. A deep sentiment Sam shares.

The natural, primeval powers shaping and shifting this land each day; the stern, polar climate that leaves but a narrow strip to sustain life humbles him. For Sam, Iceland is like a strict mother, laying down the laws so that her children may survive; cautioning them to be prudent with her gifts of abundant fish and to attend carefully to her sensitive environment's needs. As she does all over this good Earth. Yet in Iceland, the Earth Mother's warnings are impossible to ignore.

Despite the threats posed by daily tremors, possible eruptions and violent winds sweeping the island, Sam feels thoroughly grounded. Paradoxically, all these dangers give him an intense sense of security. Nature demands respect, defies dominion and the tiny human must honor her and adapt. This he believes and is grateful to have found his place on Iceland. He has come home.

FIVE

an balances four tankards on a tray, making his way to their table, "Here's to our team! Let us wash down and be done with the drama and investigations of the past two days! A toast to the happiest of endings!"

Jace, Emma and Sam pick up their glasses, shouting "To us! Skál!" They had all been under a strain since the incident with the American. Depending on the outcome of police investigations, there was still a chance that their work would be severely restricted, if not shut down completely. Now that Sigurdson has exonerated Sam and Chuck, the entire diving guide team is collectively relieved.

Teams and guides from other tour operators also lift their glasses in solidarity. Working with tourists from around the world, accidents are a professional risk. It could have been them. "Skál!" they shouted, for a moment drowning out Björk's voice vibrating from the speakers.

The Pineapple Bar is an insider's tip in downtown Reykjavik, a cozy living room where guides gather. Listed far down, when at all, in tour guides and apps, Pineapple Bar's furnishings are simple and completely devoid of any Viking accoutrements. The name alone is incongruous to Iceland, so the bar is frequented almost exclusively by locals and guides for the various tourist businesses. The long bar has a scattering of mismatched stools, the jukebox offers only Icelandic pop, rock and folk music and the few tables exude flea market flair. The neon sign above the door outside depicts a blinking pineapple, nothing more.

«We should think about opening our own business. Have you considered how much Scuba Silfra takes in in a day? Fifty or more clients each day at a hundred and eighty dollars per person, per tour," Sam quietly suggests to his three colleagues. "That comes to…wait a sec…over two hundred and fifty thousand dollars a month! And Icelandic tourism has a growth rate of over twenty percent per annum."

"You're right, of course, but what goes up, must come down," Jace comments drily.

"It certainly does," Ian interjects. "It was precisely a naïve faith in permanent growth that drove Iceland to bankruptcy during the last financial crisis."

"So, what? What do you think the Icelanders learned? That after the crisis is before the crisis, until then, business as usual" Sam laughs.

It's true. Iceland is enjoying an incredible tourism boom. Although it still draws over seventy percent of its income from fishing quotas, tourism now ranks second in national income. This year alone, three million tourists are expected, ten tourists to every Icelander and nearly all of them during the three or four spring and summer months. Amazingly enough, the flood of tourists is well-distributed outside of Reykjavik. Of course, tour busses coach sightseers over the Golden Circle Tour, congregating at major attractions like the sixty-meter high waterfall on Seljalandsfoss. But, turning only a few kilometers inland from the main coastal turnpike, you could still quietly commune with Nature without seeing a soul.

Questions, of course, arise on just how sustainable such growth is, and what impact it may have on the ecosystem's delicate equilibrium. Already a number of Icelanders are loudly demanding a limit to the influx of visitors, but this has not stopped hotels from sprouting up out of the rocky coast. There's rarely a room under four hundred euros a night and they are booked solid for the entire season. Even the Air Bed and Breakfast, where locals rent out their kid's room, are only minimally less expensive. Yet, tourists keep pouring in. Money is no object. It keeps coming in by the truckload, but it is never enough. Instead of foresight, humans are gifted with twenty-twenty hindsight and as long there's more to be had, the wheels will keep rolling.

Sam thought back on a CEO of a major Swiss bank whom he had met at the Zurich Opera Ball at the height of the financial crisis. There was plenty of not-so-discreet whispering about how he had the temerity to show up at such an elaborate affair when his bank was on the brink of disaster. Unable to ignore the criticism, the stocky bank boss, well in his cups, sat down at Sam's table.

It's the way of the world, he explained. He had known for months that he could only choose how he would fail. There was no doubt about if he would. Had he warned investors away from the high-risk U.S. real estate bonds and their utopian yields, he would have been marked as a reaction-ary coward, a relic of the past unwilling to move with the times. The only alternative was to join the vampires and suck his share of blood, sweep caution under the rug and play along until the inevitable collapse. So, of course, he chose blood-lust, careful to take the necessary measures to safeguard his private assets. Not to mention those of his political and economic cronies who then blackmailed Switzerland into bailing out system-relevant banks with taxpayers hard-earned francs.

He's right from his point of view, Sam thought back then. Once bailed out, the bank instantly returned to scoping out high-yield speculative investments. All proposed measures for installing tougher regulations to avoid a repeat performance were nipped in the bud or so diluted they were but a ripple on the surface. The vampires found fresh meat. Business as usual.

"I'm sure you're right, my friend. But do you really think the hunger for more can be satisfied?" Ian speculates, wiping beer suds from his beard.

"Not as long as we don't change our way of thinking," Emma interjects, adding, "when will they have enough? How much is enough?"

"Well, I for one could use a bit more," Sam conjectures. "A few years running a good diving business and I could retire. A bungalow in Spain maybe…"

"No yacht?" Jace laughs and they all join in, raising their glasses. "Skál!"

Ian looks up and spots someone. He rises and goes to the bar, coming back with a hollow-cheeked young man. "I would like to introduce you all to Jon Friman," and easily presses the slight figure into an empty chair before turning to get another round of beer.

Jon nods to the group of friends but does not speak. He is still wrapped in parka and woolen cap although the temperature in the Pineapple is close to tropical.

"Actually, I was just leaving, just wanted a quick beer," Jon protests when Ian places another tankard in front of him.

"What's the hurry? Have another blog to write? Is there going to be an eruption?" Ian teases. "You all should know that this young man is something of an expert. He operates a website on volcanos and earthquakes and writes what the Icelandic Meteorological Office doesn't dare to write. Am I right, my friend?"

"The MET couldn't write it, even if they wanted to. They have to go through so-called scientific channels. I'm just a hobby geologist in their books. But at least they let me do my work. So, I really have to go," Jon mumbles.

Ian gently but firmly holds his shoulder. Jon doesn't have a chance. "C'mon, tell us. What's up?"

Jon surrenders, "Okay, I don't seem to have a choice."

"Nope," Ian grins broadly.

"Well, here it is: Katla, one of our largest volcanos, is long overdue. Fifty years overdue. Over the past few days, there have been continuous quakes measuring 3.5 on the Richter scale, something the MET Office does not tell us. But what worries me more are the indications of tremors in the volcano system beneath Langjökull. You know that tremor-like quakes are the prologue to an eruption. They're like the trembling in a Parkinson's sufferer and are very much more ominous than when a tectonic plate slips a millimeter or two. Tremor-quakes occur when magma rises from the depths and forms a bubble beneath the Earth's surface. So, I want to look at the latest data."

"Beneath Langjökull? Could that effect our tours?" Emma wants to know. All of them are now leaning in to hear better over the voices and loud music. The bar is packed.

"I can't say just yet. But the thing is, when quakes occur regularly in short sequences, creating a pattern, we speak of tremors. It's as if teeth in the Earth's crust are chattering. Usually that's a warning that an eruption is imminent," Jon explains, finally slipping off his parka. He warms to his subject and captive audience.

"So why doesn't the MET Office issue warnings? My goodness! There are hundreds of tourists in that area every day, not to mention us!" Jace exclaims.

"Why do you think?" Sam interjects. "It's like the weather forecast in Swiss skiing regions. If a snowstorm is brewing and they warn people, not a soul will go on the slopes. And if the storm blows over and nothing happens, the meteorologists are nearly lynched. It's bad for business."

"Sure, but better a false alarm than fatalities!" Emma cries indignantly.

"Easy now," Ian says soothingly. "Let Jon go on."

"The MET Office really is between a rock and a hard place. There are tremors, but not consistently regular, and we had the same thing last year, but nothing happened," Jon informs them and continues, "All the same, there seems to be a connection between the tremors in the volcano system beneath Langjökull and the quakes in Katla's caldera. The two systems are over a hundred kilometers apart and we cannot figure out how they could be influencing each other. Still, if Katla erupts, it's lights out all over Iceland. An eruption would be at least fifty times more violent than the Eyjafjallajökull eruption in 2010. Remember? The volcano's ash brought European air traffic to a standstill for two weeks. Katla could knock out half of the Western hemisphere – for months."

Jaws drop all around. "And what do you think all that might imply?" Sam asks quietly.

"It means we might be looking at two systems in an eruption cycle. Something like that happened about four thousand years ago. Iceland was battered by eruptions and completely obscured by smoke and ash clouds for months. This time it implies that gigantic tsunamis, something called a lahar, made up of meltwater and mud could flood the coastal region. Langjökull alone has six-hundred-meter thick ice. If magma should melt it, well, then that's all folks."

"Holy moly!" Ian groans, "And what do you suggest we do?"

"If you're up there in Silfra and notice tangible earthquakes, then get out – and fast. Otherwise, I can only recommend you keep constant tabs on what the MET Office publishes on their website. Now, I really have to go," Jon concludes, whipping out his smartphone with one hand and picking up his parka with the other.

Still stunned, the others also reach into their pockets and swipe open their mobiles.

"Look! Alone in the time we've been sitting here there's been twenty quakes in Katla's caldera!" Emma cries out.

Jon waves goodbye to the group, but no one takes notice. They're all glued to their displays. Only Ian gets up and walks Jon to the door.

"Are you serious, man? Should we make a run for it?" Ian asks him.

"I don't know," Jon replies, shrugging his shoulders and pulling up his parka's zipper. A sharp wind sweeps through the bar when he opens the door.

"See you 'round," he says and walks off into the sunlit night.

When Ian gets back to the table, three heads turn to him, troubled looks on their faces.

"Tell me Ian, is Jon an apocalypticist?" Sam asks.

"Who knows?" Ian says and laughs. "People have been living on this island for a thousand, eight hundred years. I doubt they'll vanish tomorrow!"

Not one of them is in the mood for lighthearted entertainment anymore. On the drive back to V18 they paint doomsday pictures of what could happen. When they go inside, they find Marie, Piet, Mickey and Julia playing cards at the large kitchen table. When Ian begins to relate their conversation with Jon, all interest in the game is forgotten.

Mickey is more amused than concerned once Ian finishes his recitation. "Hey," he suggests, "it'd be great! We'll loot Vínbúðin first and then the supermarket and lock ourselves in here for the duration!" No one finds this particularly amusing. Worried faces exchange somber glances and the air is laden with uncertainty.

What if Katla really did erupt and blanket the island with ash? She's a hundred and fifty kilometers from Reykjavik as the bird flies and there's no chance of lava spewing that far. But, like

Eyjafjallajökull back then, Katla would certainly bring air traffic to a standstill, probably for weeks. Chaos. Still, the prospect of hunkering down in V18 without work for the duration would be a picnic, Sam thinks. He knows what Katla is capable of, had read up on it over the last few days. Her potential for destruction is enormous. One eruption in earlier centuries had caused a minor ice age throughout Europe and there are historians who believe the ensuing winter famine had triggered the French Revolution.

Sam is not about to broadcast this tidbit, though. His friends feel threatened enough as it is. You could cut the worry in the V18 kitchen with a knife.

SIX

Lounging trustfully on his fickle IKEA bed, Sam scrolls through his emails. It is his day off and he had planned on sleeping in, but sleeping is a challenge with the container harbor operating full blast and sharp, glaring sunlight framing the blinds over the window. It's a clear day, that much is obvious. He will go out after breakfast.

Since their night at the Pineapple, he has subscribed to Jon Friman's Iceland Geology blog. His mailbox notifies him of a new blog entry. Sam opens it and gasps.

Updates from Iceland Geology

Volcano and earthquake activity in Iceland

Edition 18/05/2018:

- *Strong earthquake swarm in Langjökull volcano system*

- *Katla expands, preparing to erupt*

This morning at 05:25, a swarm of over twenty quakes occurred in the Langjökull glacier area. Six of the quakes measured over 3.5 and the strongest, at 4.8, occurred at 5:55 am. The strong quake's epicenter was eight hundred meters below Prestahnúkur's caldera, west of the glacier.

Momentarily, all's quiet in the region. However, this tremor activity is characteristic and, in my opinion, indicates that further intense quakes or an eruption of the Prestahnúkur volcano can be expected any time.

There are no reports of damage, but the Þingvellir Tourist Center will not open until 8 am. The area is a highly popular tourist attraction and it is not yet known if authorities will close off the region.

Also recorded last night: Strong quakes in Katla's caldera in southern Iceland. The epicenter was a mere hundred meters below the ten-kilometer-wide caldera which is covered by an ice cap two to seven hundred meters thick. In my opinion, these consistent, strong tremors indicate expanding magma chambers beneath the caldera and an imminent eruption.

Between 930 and 1918 Katla has displayed more or less intensive eruptions in intervals of thirteen to fifty-nine years. The most recent did not break through the ice layer. A powerful eruption would, however, exceed the impact of Eyjafjallajökull's eruption in 2010 several times over. The *ensuing ash clouds could put an abrupt halt to Northern European air traffic for several months.*

The authorities have issued a red alert and I expect citizens living in the town of Vik, situated directly below Katla, will soon be evacuated and the Ring Street closed to traffic.

Further information to follow on this website.

All data is property of the Icelandic MET Office.

Shocked, Sam reads the text a second time. He gets out of bed and pulls up the blinds, immediately shielding his eyes. Piercing sunlight cloaks the bay, forklifts zip over the harbor and the street is full of commuters driving to work. Business as usual.

He slips into his baggy jogging pants and pads barefoot to the kitchen. Not a soul to be found, but he hears the television in the common room. Shoulder on shoulder, the entire household, except those on a tour, is crowded into the room and staring at the screen. The sagging sofa, several chairs and the floor are filled with silent, watching people.

Standing in the doorway, Sam hears, "And that closes our update on volcano and earthquake activities. We ask people to keep their radios tuned and listen for further updates."

Jace gets up and mutes the flat screen. As far as Sam can remember, the TV has never been on before. It's only used for gaming.

Answering the question on Sam's face, Jace fills him in, "Everything's under control. Apparently, there were some heavy tremors last night, but the authorities say there's no need to be concerned. They referred to similar activities last year, pointing out that there were no damages or eruptions then, so there shouldn't be this time, either."

"Okay, but have you read Jon's blog?" Sam addresses his assembled colleagues, "He assesses the situation rather differently. He writes Katla is preparing to erupt and Þingvellir Park – which means Silfra – should be closed!"

"Yeah, and we all know how eager Jon is to announce the end of the world!" Chuck calls out, reaping general laughter. "Let's have breakfast, my shift starts in an hour. Drake called a few minutes ago. Customers are lined up, it's business as usual!"

Sam stirs an instant coffee and sits down with Emma and Jace, who are shoveling muesli into their mouths and looking satisfied with the world. Sam fills his bowl with cornflakes and milk.

"Don't you think we should take a closer look at the situation? Want to join me on a jaunt to Vik?"

"Why not?" Emma agrees, "We're off today, too. But what do you hope to find?"

"We could just have a look around, take a walk on Vik's wonderful black beaches and keep our ears open. It would interest me to know if the locals are just as unconcerned."

Fifteen minutes later, they are rattling along in Sam's dilapidated red Citroën. He had bought it upon his arrival for a hundred thousand Icelandic króna, a whopping thousand U.S. dollars. It isn't much, but it gives him the freedom to explore the island on free days.

And today, Iceland is beautifully clear, not a cloud in the sky. Although the sun is shining and it's about ten degrees, a cold sharp wind keeps the warmth from penetrating. Sam, Jace and Emma take the turnpike out of Reykjavik and head East, aiming for the southernmost tip of the island. Over moss-covered lava fields glowing several shades of green and lupine lilac in the sunlight, along surreal, craggy slopes of extinct volcanos, they arrive at a monticule with a breathtaking view over the fertile plain of Selfoss.

A bit over two hours after leaving V18, the Citroën clatters into Vik í Mýrdal, a coastal town slightly southwest of Lake Heiðarvatn with Mt. Reynisfjall in the northeast, nesting place for countless Atlantic puffins and fulmars.

Vik is renowned for its black and shimmering lava sand beach. It is among the top ten most beautiful non-tropical beaches in the world. A wild and roiling ocean has tempted more than a few brazen tourists out to sea. Some lived to boast while others perished in the icy waters.

Three oddly shaped basalt sea stacks off the coast, Skessudrangur, Landdrangur and Langsamur, are collectively known as the Reynisdrangar. Legend tells of two trolls attempting to pull a three-mast ship to shore. Despite their frantic efforts at a time of year when nights are short, they have yet to reach shore when the sun appears on the horizon, immediately turning them and their ship to stone. Landdrangur made it closest to the beach, pulling his ship Langsamur behind him while Skessudrangur, Landdrangur's wife, has been abandoned farthest from the shore.

Sam sees no immediate indications of anxiety in Vik. Tourists are moseying along the beach, making selfies with Reynisdrangar in the background. Jace and Emma are among them, hugging each other close, their arms stretched out, mobiles at the ready, sea stacks behind. Sam leaves them to their billing and cooing and walks over the black sand to the restaurant.

Looking out over the parking lot he espies a fully loaded van and a Land Rover next to it. He gets himself a coke and casually strolls around the parking lot until he sees a sturdy Icelander carrying additional bags to the Land Rover.

"Hey," Sam greets him, "off for a holiday?"

"Joker," the blond giant retorts, shaking his head and continuing to load the car.

"Katla?" Sam poses a direct question.

The Icelander, who introduces himself as Ragnar, explains that everyone in Vik carries a beeper. If it should go off, that is the signal to get out of town as fast as possible.

Sam tells him he is a Silfra diving guide and they have seen the reports of recent, continuous activity, even in the past few hours.

"If I were you, I'd think twice about swimming in the canyon. It's no picnic when things get rocking down there," Ragnar advises before going to get more luggage.

Sam sees Emma and Jace scanning the parking lot, probably looking for him. He waves and indicates the restaurant terrace. Divers have a knack for wordless communication, their minds tuning into another wavelength the moment speech is no longer possible.

Moments later, they are sitting on the terrace, steaming cappuccinos cooling on the table. Sunglasses protect their eyes from the brilliant sun as they gaze out over the incredibly beautiful black beach, hypnotized by the wildly churning ocean. Just as Sam raises his cup to his lips, a resounding crack tears through the air, the sound of concrete bursting. The small table begins to shiver, as if cold. Then it's over.

Sam carefully puts his cup down and the trembling starts up again, much colder this time, rattling the cups on their saucers. What sounds like mighty thunder echoes down from the mountains at their backs followed by a series of crackles and detonations like splintering ice floes in springtime. And then silence. Dead silence. Not a person moves, not a breath stirs. Someone had hit the pause button on the video of life. People walking on the beach have frozen mid-stride. On the restaurant terrace cups are half raised. Eyes are fixed on the ocean, on the mountains, on each other, but no one and nothing moves. Even the seagulls are silent, sailing in soundless circles. Emma and Jace look at one another, eyebrows raised. It seems like an eternity to Sam. The world is on hold, waiting. But for what? Nothing happens, and people gradually arouse from their paralysis, begin to chatter or swipe their cellphones, texting, searching.

"Wow," Emma comments drily, "looks like the news wasn't telling the whole story." It seems everyone is still waiting, like firework spectators on the Fourth of July, holding their breath for the grand finale. But nothing happens. The Earth is still. Ominously so.

"That calls for a round on the house!" Ragnar announces, coming out on the terrace with a tray full of glasses, offering schnapps all around, avidly declaring that was normal in these parts. Welcome to Iceland!

Guests crowd around Ragnar, taking shot glasses and talking excitedly. Ragnar shoots Sam a look, imperceptibly shaking his head and pointing discreetly to his beeper hanging mute at his belt.

Jace drains his cup and suggests, "Maybe we should get going, what do you guys think?"

"You mean before the alarm is sounded and everyone runs for their cars as if the devil himself is on their heels, hopelessly blocking the Ring Road?" Sam translates with a wink. Jace merely nods and Emma's face is suddenly drained of all color. Behind her two friends, she sees a thin column of smoke rising.

Sam sticks bank notes under his coffee cup and the three of them make for the car. A plump American at the table next to theirs, comments, "Those are guides, I believe. Why are they leaving so abruptly?" When Sam glances back, he notices an overall move toward departure, backpacks are slung over and buckled, tabs are paid, wallets, purses and jackets firmly closed.

Sam guides the Citroën carefully over the gravel road that leads onto Ring Road. Jace and Emma are staring at their cellphones.

"That was two tremors, both over 4.0, according to the Icelandic MET Office homepage," Jace grumbles and Emma adds, "Yeah, and over the last hour Langjökull also had a swarm of more than thirty quakes, one of them over 5."

"Over 5?" Sam interjects. "Let's just hope Silfra's canyon walls hold up! Damn, this sounds like serious business."

Speeding back to Reykjavik, they give no thought to the scenery but discuss what is foremost in their minds.

"The authorities have everything under control," Jace propounds. "They will get word out in time if it proves necessary and take the right steps. After all, they have hundreds of gaging stations and employ a veritable army of geologists drawing on two hundred years of scientific data. It is not the first time the Earth's crust has gotten restless without becoming violent. And remember eight years ago, when Eyjafjallajökull erupted, the authorities warned people in time and no one was hurt."

"Like everywhere else on the planet, the authorities are controlled by politicians and finances. Even the weather reports in Switzerland are censored," Sam replies, squinting in the glaring sun, trying to maneuver his car around potholes left over from last winter. "As sure as death and taxes, Iceland's geologists are not going to risk the tourist season. Broadcasting warnings of an imminent, massive volcano eruption triggering earthquakes, landslides and ice tsunamis that will swallow the valley when the glaciers melt is not what I would call enticing advertising. And then there's the people here. What will you do when panic breaks out and everyone storms the airport trying to save their skin? The airlines are booked to the last seat anyway. The last thing Iceland's government wants is news reports and social media posts on mass hysteria making the rounds,"

"But really," Emma protests, "do you think images of thousand dying in a volcano eruption are more attractive?"

"No," Sam cedes, "but the damage would already have been done. The world community will forget it ever happened in a few weeks, a month at most. It's the same with terrorist attacks. And rebuilding the infrastructure will take some time anyway. A false alarm would be just as devastating for business. How would you decide? Would you take the risk of causing millions in damages to the tourist business, allowing several hundred bankruptcies? And it turns out to be a false alarm? Or would you wait?"

"I simply can't believe that people are so obsessed with money," Jace exclaims. "That's insane! We are talking about human life here! We're talking about our lives!"

Sam turns his head slightly with one eye on the road and the other on Jace, "And yet, my friend, that's how it is. Humanity is insane. Just look at what we have done to our planet."

SEVEN

When the trio gets back to V18, there seems to be some kind of conference underway in the kitchen. Tara and Drake are sitting on the arms of their chairs, leafing through computer prints.

"We've consulted the authorities again this morning and although there is a high alert level, they are not taking measures to evacuate or block access to Þingvellir Park. They ensure us that the situation is being watched closely around the clock," Drake announces.

"We just got back from Vik í Mýrdal, and I can tell you, there's some heavy activity going on there, we even saw smoke rising from Katla," Jace bursts out.

"You were mistaken. There really was a swarm of heavy tremors in Katla's caldera today, but the smoke wasn't from Katla. What you saw was a transformer. They supply antennas and gaging stations with electricity and this one didn't survive the tremors," Tara sets the record straight.

"And what does all this mean for us?" Sam asks, stepping up to his bosses.

"Have a seat first, Sam," Drake offers firmly. "It's true, Katla could be dynamite. There are strong tremors that could indicate a forthcoming eruption, but it is the third time in recent years that she's played cat and mouse with geologists, without it coming to anything. Even if Katla did erupt, we would only be inconvenienced. Of course, that would end the tourist season and we might be stuck here for a while with air traffic disabled, but that's would be the worst of it. No big deal."

"And Þingvellir?" Sam wants to know.

"That's what I was trying to explain when you guys came in," Drake sighs. "Let's go at it again from the beginning." Chuck turns to the new arrivals with his arms clasped across his chest and demonstratively rolls his eyes for all to see.

Drake continues, "As you all know, over the last few days and even hours, there have been several quake swarms at Langjökull, some which could be felt in Silfra. This afternoon, around the time the impacts at Katla occurred, there were another twenty shocks, none of them, however, over 3.0. We joined the rangers and tested Silfra's walls. Everything is stable, which gives us the all-clear to continue our tours. Still we have taken precautions and installed an alarm telephone. The rangers will inform us immediately if we need to interrupt the tour or get out of there fast."

"And what does Jon Friman say to all of this?" Emma asks, prompting a snigger from Chuck.

"Jon might be a geologist with a blog, but he has no authority to recommend safety measures," Tara replies, grinning.

"That's not what I meant," Emma corrects her. "I meant what does he say about what's going on?"

"He has been issued an official warning. If he doesn't stop publishing doomsday fantasies, they will shut down his website," Chuck lets them know. "He only wants his five minutes of fame, so people will subscribe to his website and thinks he'll get it by promising an apocalypse!"

Sam looks up from his cellphone, "Well, it seems to have worked, he hasn't posted anything new since this morning."

"Hah!" Chuck grins, throwing back his head and swiping his long fringe out of his face.

"Now that that's cleared up, business as usual. Just keep tabs on updates in the WhatsApp group. I'll keep you informed. So, back to work for all of you with shifts," Drake finishes, rising from his seat.

Tara and Drake distribute a few pats on the back before disappearing in the office. Customers are waiting.

The meeting dissolves. Piet shuffles off toward the showers in his flipflops, a towel around his waist. Barbu and Simi rummage around in their locker for something edible. Emma is just standing there lost in thought, her body language whispers uncertainty, her freckles seem darker in her pale face. She comes back to the kitchen, "Pasta?" she says to the room at large. Sam and Jace simply nod without looking up, their eyes glued to their cellphones.

Marie takes a seat next to Sam. Studying his smartphone intently, he fails to notice her at first. She scoots her chair closer to his, plants her elbows in the humus of breadcrumbs and other debris on the table and gives Sam a sidelong glance. Sam perceives the scraping chair, gets a whiff of something delicious and he looks up, zooming in on her dark brown eyes. Marie's face is less than two hands' breadth from his. She scans Sam's face curiously and something in her eyes unsettles him.

He is suddenly reminded of his days as a no-
madic manager. Of the times he would join fellow
business mercenaries in playing a bar game called
how long have you been here? All of them earned
their money or spurs in the twilight zone between
one economically weak country and the next.
Building business. The game's rules were simple
and based on an observation they all had made.

Whenever a foreigner entered a pub, a swarm
of local women immediately encircled him. It had
happened to all of them at some point, although
Sam could never figure out how women knew the
man was a newcomer. It seemed as if they could
smell something unique about him, or maybe he
radiated a novice's uncertainty.

Anyway, the more experienced men would
speculate on how long the man had been in the
city. They watched his reactions to the women. If
his eyes lit up and he offered to buy one or two a
drink, he couldn't possibly have been there more
than a day or two. But if he smiled, patted a female shoulder here, a cheek there and turned to
the bar while waiting for a table, he knew the
ropes and had been around at least a week,
maybe two. Once estimates had been made, they
would ask the man directly. The least accurate
guess paid the next round of drinks.

European men are always blindsided when woman approach them directly in a bar. It just isn't done where they come from. A man could sit in a European bar for weeks without a woman taking any notice of him. Depending, of course on the type of bar it is, but that is a whole different can of worms. The women here were seriously shopping for a European or American husband, someone to take them away to a better life. They were motivated by the prospect of being loved and gave their potential futures thorough inspections, both intensely probing and charmingly naïve.

Is he courteous and kindly? Can he take care of her? Is he rich and generous? Is he single? Is he worthy of her love and can she depend on him, maybe even have children? Of course, Sam was also taken in at first, was flattered and agreed to a series of rendezvous. He quickly discovered that flowers were a mandatory offering, and in his eyes proof of the reigning naiveté. Yet, when he asked his chosen darling what she would like to do that weekend, she answered indignantly that he was the man, he should decide, whatever he chose to do, she would love to be with him. An unprecedented validation of his manliness. The frequency and similarity of tales such as his own told by colleagues soon made clear to him the intention behind the innocent submission and infinite flattery.

The women wanted a husband now. The men, though, were willing to take their time. If a man was too hesitant, the lady dropped him and turned her sights on the next prospect, gazing deeply and invitingly into his eyes.

What interest lies behind Marie's beautiful dark brown eyes? His interest in the news and updates on Iceland's volcanic activity fades into the background. When she lays a hand on his shoulder, he slips his mobile into his shirt pocket. She turns to face him and gently strokes his cheek. Sam's heart takes a leap, leaving his stomach in turmoil. He would love to say something charming but cannot seem to fill his mouth with intelligible words.

His suspicions are blown away like shredded clouds in Icelandic wind. He is here, in Iceland and his days in Eastern Europe are long gone.

From day one she has fascinated him, since the moment she opened her mouth and introduced herself in English, the common language here, her French accent giving simple words a whole new dimension. Incredibly sexy to Sam's ears. They have already worked a few snorkeling tours together and Sam couldn't help casting covetous glances at her muscular body when she climbed into her suit. And each time he helped her with the zipper that runs across and up the back of her bloodred dry suit, he had the surreal sensation he was zipping up a breathtaking evening gown. During the final security check, he must repress the impulse to reach around and kiss her neck as she sweeps up her hair to close the neck cuff. Gearing up is an intensely physical experience.

Of course, he doesn't stand a chance. In her mid-thirties, Marie is an extremely attractive woman. Like a flowering willow tree in springtime, every single male guide – young Adonis' to a man – in V18 swarms to taste her nectar. She can take her pick of escorts for any bar tour in Reykjavik and when she shows signs of tiring, at least three or four men begin to yawn demonstratively. Sam, twenty years her senior, a small paunch and shaved head could not possibly be viewed as a serious rival. Still, when it's just the two of them in the van traveling to or from a tour, they enjoy splendid conversation. Marie seemed truly interested when he told her of his experiences as a company leader and adventures as an industrial mercenary. His extensive knowledge of philosophical works, history and natural sciences; his life views impress her, or so he believes. Sometimes she would lay her arm across his shoulder as they talk, and driving would suddenly become an effort. Once, she had even pressed a kiss on his cheek when he had unpacked her gear box and hung her suit over the heater to dry. But that was just a gesture of gratitude. Her behavior mystifies him.

But, maybe, just maybe, his intelligence turns her on much more than a flawless physique. The thought ignites a spark of hope in Sam's mind. Maybe she really is attracted to him. Or, he reasons with his libido, it's probably just her cultural background, her French congeniality. He's seen her cuddle up to other colleagues, both male and female, or lay an arm over someone's shoulders. He mustn't enlarge reality.

Now, he is sitting there like an adulating schoolboy whose goddess, the beautiful, popular girl two classes up, suddenly pulls him into her circle of light. A tender touch at his ankle makes him look down. Her naked foot has slipped from her sandal and is gently rapping. She is wearing tight boxer shorts and her firm brown thighs smell of flowers. She must have just come from the shower, her damp hair still carrying the slight sulfur odor from Iceland's warm water. Sam throws a shy, split-second glance at her baggy, faded tank-top, obviously washed a hundred times, hanging loosely on her rounded shoulders. If he had the nerve to look at her for more than two seconds at a time, he could easily take a peek at her belly button through the round neck.

Get a grip! He reins himself in. What am I doing? What a cliché! Am I hot for her or am I falling in love? Be still, my beating heart, enjoy the view and leave it at that. She's a wonderful woman, but do you really think you could have a serious relationship? You are much too old for her!

"We're teamed up tomorrow, mon cheríe. Are you worried?" Marie asks him, not ten centimeters from his face.

"Hmmm," is the best he can manage. Convinced she's only interested in any information he might have to share, pulls his cellphone out of his pocket. The moment passes. Marie sits back and upright in her chair, questioning him with her eyes.

"It's just that I suspect the decision-makers are playing a dangerous game. Sure, there's a lot of money at stake, but so are our lives," Sam gesticulates with his mobile.

Emma places the pot of pasta on the table and fills plates for the four of them. Sam takes a few surviving beer cans from this shelf on the fridge.

"A toast to our last supper," Sam comments with a wry grin.

They shovel their fusilli and tomato sauce in the oddly silent and empty kitchen. The sounds of plate-scraping, chewing and swallowing are uncomfortably loud. The kitchen is usually bustling at this time of day, returning shifts cooking lunch and late shifts having breakfast. Stories are exchanged, and jokes told while the plates pile up in the sink, the occasional clink giving the general cacophony a melodic touch.

Simi and Barbu have taken their full pates into the common room where it seems nearly everyone else has gathered, punishing the defeated sofa and ottomans into service while they wordlessly watch the news channel.

Sam does his stint at the sink while Emma and Jace say good night. At seven in the evening! Even for those two lovebirds it was early. Maybe the day's events brought out their need for intimacy.

Chuck is sitting half obscured in shadows at one of the rear tables. Sam observes him steadily gazing at Marie as she leaves the kitchen. Sam watches her, too and when she is gone, the two men's eyes meet. For a moment, Sam believes he sees an aggressive spark in Chuck's eyes, but Chuck grins at him and shakes his fingers as if he had touched something very hot, giving Sam a short nod. Sam nods back and returns to the dishes.

Drying his hands on a dish towel, Sam finishes in the kitchen and heads for the shower, letting the warm water rain down on him for a good fifteen minutes.

Feeling not the slightest desire to join in on the discussions and speculations in the windowless common room, he goes to his closet kingdom and closes the door. He raises the blinds and gazes out the window, opening it to fish out one of his favorite beers from the plastic bag swaying in the wind. His private stock of Einstök – Icelandic pale ale, one down, nine to go. The wind had picked up and the dark clouds racing over the bay promised horizontal rainfall.

Just as he kicks his flipflops under the bed and settles down on the mattress, there's a discreet knock at his door. Sam gets up, pulling the bath towel tightly around his waist, and opens the door a crack.

"Am I disturbing you?" Marie is standing in the hallway, a can of Einstök in her hand and grins when she sees Sam's get-up.

"Not a bit," Sam mumbles. "Come on in. I'll just throw some clothes on."

He opens the door to his cupboard, hoping it offers a bit of protection and can't help but smile to himself at his youthful modesty. Taking his fisher-pants he had bought in Thailand he slips them on and ties the waist strings. Bare-chested, he sits down on the bed where Marie has already made herself comfortable. There are no chairs.

Marie gives him the once-over, grins and raises her beer can, "You're in damned good shape for your age." Sam eyes her skeptically. "I mean, I wanted to say you're in good shape," she corrects herself and they both laugh.

"I came to ask you what you think of the situation. Obviously, you are taking it more seriously than the others and since you're anything but a yellow-belly, I find that worrying," Marie explains her visit, placing one impeccable thigh on the bed so she can face Sam. He does the same and looks her in the eye for the first time since she entered the room. She takes his breath away. He watches his composure walk out of the room. Marie's proximity, her aura and her presence in his most private space; the intimacy of the two of them on his bed. He swallows and struggles to save face.

"What?" Marie asks impishly, sensing the impact she makes on him.

"Well, you're in damned good shape yourself," he counters, grinning and mysteriously enough this brings his composure back under his skin.

"Gee, thanks – now tell me!" She commands. So that's it, Sam thinks, she's here about the earthquakes. She is out for his mind, not his body, which relaxes and disappoints him at the same time. He is now relieved he had not given himself away in the kitchen. He nearly had.

"I can't say I know any more than anyone else," he begins hesitantly.

"Sure, but you aren't so gullible. C'mon, don't keep me in suspense. After all, I have to go in the water with you tomorrow," she says, giving him a playful punch in the chest.

"Don't worry about that. I promise not to embarrass you," he laughs and taps his beer can on hers.

"But, seriously, what I saw and heard and felt in Vik today with Emma and Jace was pretty damn frightening. There was this incredibly loud clap as if ancient stones were suddenly bursting. And the birds fell deathly silent. Not a peep. Then the thundering, like a massive storm far below the Earth's surface. As if a giant troll was waking up down there from an age-long sleep, stretching and knocking about."

"You're a veritable poet!"

"Stop teasing," he laughs again and then becomes serious once more.

"But what I learned from Jon Friman is spookier. He told me that Katla is long overdue and he believes an eruption is inevitable."

"Hmm, I heard that, too," Marie confirms. "Did he say anything about Langjökull and the quakes in Þingvellir Park?"

"He thinks one of the volcanos in the system there could also erupt or trigger heavy earthquakes or even a lahar."

"What is a lahar?" Marie asks, eyes widening.

"A lahar is a mud and debris flow that occurs when the intense heat of rising magma explodes into ancient ice, melting it violently. It is likened to an inland tidal wave consisting of rock, scree and water and depending on the terrain's gradient, a lahar can reach a velocity of over a hundred and ten kilometers per hour, its path stretching as far as a hundred kilometers, flooding huge areas. And it can be hot. Up to ninety-five degrees Celsius," Sam explains, enjoying the awe in Marie's eyes. Ever since his teens, he had taken great pleasure in terrifying the objects of his desire with tales of horror. It offered him the perfect opening to play Sir Galahad.

"Not so scintillating when you're snorkeling with a group in Silfra. Chuck and the others say Jon is a doomsday prophet. Maybe he is, maybe he isn't. If you read earlier blogs, he has often predicted eruptions that didn't happen. And when Eyjafjallajökull exploded, he, oddly enough, claimed it was only tectonic shifts and not magma. I don't know what to believe, but that doesn't mean we have to believe the worst."

Sam shrugs his shoulders and Marie lays her head on his left one.

"I don't know either, but I have a strange feeling and sometimes, I'm really afraid," she whispers.

Sam sits bolt upright and still as stone. This is the moment his knight in shining armor is supposed to take the stage, but there is only hesitation and uncertainty. After a moment he carefully lays his arm around her. "Me, too," he whispers back.

She turns her head and looks him in the eye.

Sam feels like he is falling into the depths of her nutbrown eyes. An eternity passes. He holds her in his arms, simply gazing at her face; at the tiny laughter lines around her eyes; at the small brown freckles and miniscule scars adorning her nose. Her still damp hair caresses his lower arm.

A gentle fire ignites between Marie's thighs coupled with misgivings. What is happening here? Is she in the process of seducing the bearded babe, as everyone calls Sam behind his back?

Sam's evident shyness with the opposite sex inspired the nickname. They have all seen him squirm uncomfortably when female customers compliment him. Or the time a sturdy Icelandic beauty so brazenly and persistently flirted with him that he finally fled to the men's room. What will they call her when they find out what's going on here? Cradle robber? Hardly.

She is well aware of her own reputation as a good-time girl since she's already had two affairs since she's been in Iceland. She nearly fell in love with another colleague but caught herself just in time when she realized how unreliable he is. That was a major turn-off.

So what if she explores the bearded babe a little bit? Older men are reputed to be excellent lovers.

Marie puts away her doubts, and pulls herself closer to Sam, snuggling into his arm. It's so quiet, as if they are waiting for some kind of signal.

The moment Sam senses her muscles shifting to rise, he sweeps a stray hair from her face, gently caressing her cheek. He studies her eyes, her narrow nose, her sensual mouth, the hairline above her brow and the tiny, protruding curls prefacing her mane. Marie lays her hand on his neck and pulls him close, her eyes locked on his, she stops a hair's breadth from her lips and closes her eyes.

Sam touches her upper lip ever-so gently with his own and her body falls soft and pliable in his arms. He feels his loins, hot and pulsating.

A knock at the door. "Sam? Are you asleep?" Chuck's deep voice calls softly.

Marie's body tenses. They look at each other. Should he answer? The door is not locked. What if Chuck barges in and sees them together in Sam's bed?

Sam places his finger on his lips and then on Marie's, shaking his head. Marie nods almost imperceptibly, as if Chuck could hear her move. They listen intently, hear soft music and the usual murmuring, occasionally interrupted by a laugh. Nothing exceptional.

"Sam?" Chuck calls again, this time a bit closer, as if he has his mouth to the door. They stare at the doorknob as it slowly turns and wait for the formidable click, their bodies rigid with tension. After what seems like minutes, the knob turns back to its original position and they hear the shuffling of house shoes moving slowly away.

Marie heaves a sigh of relief and sinks onto Sam's chest. That is the last thing she needs, Chuck and Sam at odds over her!

"Apparently, you are missed," Sam whispers, laughing.

"Why me? He is looking for you!"

Sam grins. He is delighted to be the one holding Marie in his arms, the lovely Frenchwoman every man in the place would give his eye teeth to be holding. He lowers his head and looks into her eyes, "Of course he is, now!" Marie can see the imp in his iris. The bearded babe is all grown up and Marie feels the arms of a man around her. A man who wants her. That's nothing new, but something is. Surprised, she consults her senses. The feel of her head on his shoulder; the smell of him; the glow of his eyes; the sound of his heart in her ear and her heart's response. She is stunned. She wants to be here and be here and be here. This is more than fun and games. Sam is a new horizon and she finds herself reaching out to him. He's different from the other men she has been this close to. There's nothing excessively adventurous about him, even though he is a talented, enthusiastic diver. He is certainly not a skirt-chaser, which makes him all the more attractive. And sexy!

An unknown, intense desire takes hold of her. She wants this man. She wants his body, his heart and his soul and she is willing to surrender herself to him to get it. She closes her eyes, pulls Sam to her and kisses him on the mouth, searching for the reasons why he wants her, desires her. Something primal opens in her, something she's kept locked up all her life. Tonight, she lets go, flings open the doors, and stays put.

Volcanos and avalanches are forgotten. Here, on this fourth-class bed where countless divers and adventurers have laid their heads, in this stark room, friction rises as it does on the tectonic plates, and the tension released causes her planet to shake.

Marie's kisses become more demanding, pressing insistently on his mouth, her tongue asking entry. He obliges, and the dam breaks as they unleash their passion. Falling back on the bed, they are impatient to explore every inch of each other's body. Their lips engaged, she pulls her tank-top up to her neck, kissing his lips, face, eyes and mouth and in the shortest of moments. Sam slips the top over her head. Bare chest to bare chest, skin on skin.

Sam strokes her warm back, his finger light on her goosebumps. She holds his head in her hands sucking and licking his mouth like a delicious ice-cream cone. He feels her firm breasts on his pounding heart, how her nipples harden and hotly stroke his skin.

They look at each other, listen to their pulsating breath.

Marie's eyes are nearly liquid black. The certainty that this time she can fully surrender flows through every fiber of her body. Never before has she felt such trust in a lover. A completely new sense of being held, of being cared for burns in her heart. It's true, older men have qualities that younger men must first grow into. She hadn't even trusted her father so completely, a man most present in his absence, with little interest in his daughter.

"This is it," Sam's mind warns him. He gazes at Marie. He has no hesitations about sleeping with such a desirable woman. He hasn't a whisper of regret as he had in younger years, following lust more faithfully than reason. His passion for Marie is boundless, his body hungry. But he also yearns for more. His battered, experienced heart hesitates.

He recalls Bruna and shies from repeating the same mistake. Will he have the courage this time? Or will he hurt Marie as he had Bruna, not to mention the damage he did to his own heart?

Marie senses his confusion, opens her eyes and questions him silently, biting her lower lip. She shifts her body to sit pelvis to pelvis on his lap, gently pushing him down on the bed.

Sam strokes her warm belly and back, his hands flat on her skin, circling, caressing, sliding up to her breasts and back down and around, rhythmically. He feels her muscles tighten and relax, surrendering to this touch, yet alive with desire. His hands rise up and tenderly grasp her breasts, his

fingers flicking back and forth over her stiff nipples. Marie moans softly and falls back on top of
him.

With a crack, the slats under the mattress snap
out of position, the mattress sinks and Marie lands
with her breasts in Sam's face.

"This is some high-class place you've got
here," she purrs. Sam hardly notices. He takes her
breasts in his hands again, circling, circling their
smooth firmness. He takes one and then the other
in his mouth, back and forth, sucking her sensitive
nipples, spiraling with his tongue. He inhales
deeply her exciting aroma, pulls her closer with his
arms and releases her again to find another secret
place for his lips and tongue.

As if rehearsed a million times, they help each
other slip out of pants, shorts and panties.

Finally, free of all barriers, Marie takes his hands
and wraps them around her hips, holding her just
above his pulsating member. They find a rhythm,
breathing in and out together. She buries her nails
in his chest, her skull is tingling, and shocks of lust
roll down her back. It's not Sam's muscles or
broad shoulders that turn her on, she's had a
bodybuilder or two beneath her hands. It is the
strength emanating from his chest that penetrates

her core. His passion, strength and solidity absorb her fervor, take in her lust with joy. He is man enough to let her take the lead and she teases the tip of his penis before gliding down, enveloping him completely. Sam moans and closes his eyes. She rides him gently, building up to a wild gallop, with his hands firmly on her hips, guiding, holding and releasing her all at once. At the climax their eyes lock.

Slowly, Marie settles on Sam's chest. Her thighs slide down over his. Her body jerking slightly as lightning bolts course through her. The storm passing. But Sam's desire is reawakening and with it her own. "Magma is rising in the caldera, tremors have begun," she whispers, and presses her trembling body on his. Raising her hips. she slowly settles on top of him, taking the full length of him inside her. Tightly intertwined, Sam churns beneath Marie's rhythmic movements in the caldera of his bed. He is swept up in the vortex and surrenders to eruption.

Neither of them feels the tremor passing through V18.

EIGHT

S am is sitting on the edge of the open van. He checks his watch. Nearly six pm. What's keeping them? He is waiting on a Golden Circle Tour group. The tour's grand finale is snorkeling in the Silfra Crack. They are already a half an hour late. It's always the same with these Asians, he mutters to himself, they probably had to stop to buy a fresh memory card. The Golden Circle Tour stops at the geyser and at Gullfoss, a golden shimmering waterfall that gives the tour its name. A magnet for photo fanatics.

He has a date with Marie and wants to be back at V18 by eight. They plan to go out for pizza. It will be the first time he has her to himself since she snuck out of his room at dawn three days ago to get ready for their joint shift. A gentle fire ignites in his loins with each memory of their lovemaking and spreads upwards, heating his chest.

This new, burgeoning warmth brings home how accustomed he has become to the permafrost directly under his skin. When diving, the suits protect them from the freezing water, but neoprene does not breathe and the thermal suits beneath retain moisture. So, standing around in damp clothes during an Icelandic summer – misty rain, gusting winds and occasional sunshine – shivers are just one or two degrees away.

But the heat in his belly goes far to heat his body – and even more so, his heart. It reminds him of the cold in his life, of the damp, unmet need for intimacy. Yet, with any saving grace, like coming into warmth and comfort after so many years in the cold, it also brings a dull fear. He could be shown the door anytime. And there's a blizzard outside. Sam smiles to himself, is he falling in love? Is that what he wants? To get hurt, again? To make a fool of himself, again? Is he arrogant enough to believe a young lady with her entire life before her would fall for an old guy like him? He's been there, done that. With Bruna. But no, he was the one who left her warmth for the cold. It had been his choice alone.

On their tour that he now calls the day after, she was warm-hearted, but aloof. Sam understood that she wanted to side-step the inevitability of Chuck's boisterous, tactless comments. He would rather not be the butt of his coarse humor, either. If there is anything to joke about. He's so sure. Maybe it was fear of the possible threat or simply curious lust that inspired her to sink into his arms. Quite possible! Since then, both Langjökull and Katla have kept their peace, aside from a few smaller swarms and negligible quakes. Nothing unusual in a country registering over a thousand small tremors each week. Maybe the authorities were right in explaining that the tectonic plates had shifted and now that the tension is released, things will go back to normal. The continental plates will continue to sporadically tremble and that's it.

Maybe their lovemaking was just an eruption of the sexual tension between them? Sam couldn't say, but he knows, for his part, that he is head over heels. He can't think of anything but Marie, Marie, Marie.

Where are they? He wants to get back, so he can find out where he stands.

He gives the sky a disgruntled look. Great, it's going to rain soon and if the wind doesn't drop, they'll have a real party stuffing shivering Chinese into dry suits.

The van's thermometer displays eleven degrees. Mild, actually, but Sam feels a bit chilled. His doubts and questions have blown out the inner fire. Since his incident with the American, the Tourism Ministry has stopped all diving tours until further notice. They need a grace period to discuss and lay down new safety regulations in the hopes of averting any further near-miss dramas. They have Sam's wholehearted support. He hasn't quite emotionally digested his brush with death and his body obviously still carries the memory of hypothermia. He is perfectly happy guiding snorkeling tours as long as it takes to clear things up, there's less risk of undercooling.

Where the hell are the Chinese?

Piet, his Dutch partner for the tour, is loitering by the buxom park ranger's vehicle, hoping to score an Icelander and check it off his list of conquests.

Although, Piet does not strike him as that kind of guy. He's a good man. Seems to have had a shitty childhood, from what he told Sam a few weeks ago on their way to a tour. His mom was a weak soul with evident physical charms. She was constantly bringing home men, confident that this time she had found a permanent father figure for her only son. But none of them had any interest in the job. They would hang around for a week or two and feast on his mother's bounteous body, getting out while the getting was good. At sixteen, Piet was fed up, unable to bear the burden of his mom's helplessness any longer and left home. He began to study psychology, but lack of funds forced him to drop out during his fourth semester. He took a job as a logistics manager. During one of his annual vacations, he tried out diving and was immediately addicted. He left his job and spent the greater part of his savings training for his diving instructor license. It was not an unusual story. Most diving instructors came to their calling over winding, rocky roads. Sam was no exception.

Sam watches Piet casually lean on the ranger's Land Rover holding a lively conversation with its occupant. Finally, the minivan pulls into the parking lot, horn blasting. At last!

Sam gets in the tour van to take care of the paperwork while Piet is in the gear van pulling out the smaller diving suits and thermal overalls to fit diminutive Asians. They are eager to get through the last tour of the day, knowing it will not take long once they are in the water. Even Silfra Scuba's extra small suits were intended for European sizes, not Asian ones. Sure, they keep them dry, but Sam's experience has proven that among the countless tourist groups he has led, Asians tend to freeze more quickly, are undercooled faster and begin to tremble within minutes. As long as they get their photos, though, they're happy. Then, he and Piet can pack it in for the day.

Documents read and signed, Sam staples them and gets out of the van. They can now get the group suited up. At that moment, between steps, a dull rumbling echoes over the plateau. Sam looks up in dismay, not now! The last thing they need is a thunderstorm. Suddenly, he finds himself reeling. What was that? Before he could formulate the thought, his body knew. A second tremor shook the parking lot and simultaneously, every van's alarm went off, making a horrendous racket.

He turns toward Silfra and is suddenly on his backside, along with everyone else around him. Earthquake! The ground begins to heave and crack, the thundering sound of ice bursting shakes their bones. Sam recognizes it from their trip to Vik. Squeaking and creaking, a thousand finger-nails over an immense chalkboard. Deafening claps of thunder and Sam looks up into the sky, unbelieving what his senses tell him and certain the cacophony can only come from the heavens. But all he sees are dark, shredded clouds hugging the mountain sides. Another monster-train barrels beneath his legs and Sam's tailbone bounces, sending tremors to skull and toes.

As if on signal, people jump into action. The Chinese run screaming back into the minivan, their ashen driver is rooted to the spot, ringing his hands in horror. Sam signals him to get the hell out of there and he jumps in the van and roars off, wheels screaming. Following the herd instinct, other cars follow suit, racing to Ring Road.

Sam looks for Piet, who, pale and addled, is struggling to disengage himself from under a mass of dry suits.

All other teams are on tours, either still in Silfra, in the lagoon or making their way back to the parking lot – Mickey and Julia, Jace and Emma with Chuck as well as Barbu and Simi – their friends.

Ian sprints toward them, his face deeply flushed, eyes wide, "We need help! Silfra is collapsing, some people are buried – call for help!" he screams from afar. A veritable giant, Ian stumbles to Sam, bends over gasping, bracing himself with his hands on his knees. His breath whistles, he coughs and spits, utterly depleted from the sprint in complete diving gear weighing at least forty kilos. Ian opens his mouth several times, spit dribbles over his beard and his terror-filled eyes flicker like a candle about to go out. He tries but cannot speak.

Sam presses his cellphone in Ian's hand without missing a stride. Ian nods and Sam races off to Silfra, Piet at his side. They grab the twisted railing on the entry platform as the Earth roars and rears up again, hurling boulders and loose debris into Silfra, transforming the canyon's mirror-smooth surface into a roiling, churning vortex.

"No one can survive that," Piet shouts at him. "They're all dead!" Sam turns to the mighty thunder rumbling at his back. A column of smoke is rising from Langjökull glacier. Heaven help us! If things weren't disastrous enough, fifty kilometers to the north of them a volcano is preparing to erupt. Sam glares at the glacier, willing himself to wake up from this nightmare. What he's seeing just cannot be happening. Stuff like this only happens in computer-generated Hollywood disaster movies. He blinks, hoping the next time he opens his eyes, he will wake up and the majestic glacier would appear, beautiful, pale and blue.

"We have to get out of here – now!" Piet yells in his face, turning from Langjökull to Silfra to Sam and back again like a frenzied cuckoo clock figure. Sam senses the Earth's delirious ferocity. He turns idiotically in a circle looking for one slice of this world that is not in the processes of devouring itself.

"We have to see where they are," Sam shouts back and climbs up on a boulder where he has a full view of the area. Piet follows trembling, his panic only overridden by his loyalty.

Lake Þingvallavatn, into which Silfra flows, is a roiling eddy, as if God or whoever has pulled the plug in a giant bathtub. Silfra's naturally quiet waters have become a raging river pouring into the lake. Silently, a raft of ducks is flying up and down the lake's shore, seeking safety and finding none. A colossal whirlpool is gathering momentum, sucking the massive waters into the Earth's thirsty maw.

Cracking and creaking break out again around them and the boulder beneath them trembles. Piet and Sam instinctively fall into a squat, their fingers finding cracks and clawing into them. A crunching sound is followed by a sharp clap of a giant's hands as he rubs them is glee. Another explosion and the hands are still. For two eternal seconds, the two tiny humans gaze into each other's enormous eyes, panting. They hunker down on the stone and wait for the next shock. They hear water rushing, rocks falling and the crunch of sliding stone. Although the Earth is still, they hold onto each other's arms and slowly rise. Knees knocking, they sway as if on a narrow plank over an abyss, consumed with acrophobia not daring to move or breath.

On his left, over Piet's shoulder Sam sees Chuck running with two snorkelers in tow, Barbu, Simi, Jace and Emma close behind. But where are the twenty other tourists? Where are Mickey and Julia?

Sam jumps down from the boulder, naively trusting the ground beneath him and sprints toward the group on the path leading from the exit platform to the parking lot. He finds them bent over, bracing themselves on their knees, heaving and gasping. Not even an athlete in top form could make it more than a hundred meters in the heavy gear.

"Where are the others?" Sam bellows.

"They didn't have a chance!" Chuck presses out between gasps. "The current pulled them into the eddy. Mickey and Julia are probably buried beneath the rubble, they were bringing up the rear in Silfra while our group was paddling around in the lagoon."

"We only got out because we were ahead of them," Jace pants, "we were already on the exit platform."

"All we could do is stand there and watch them get sucked up in the current and pulled into the lake," Emma sobs, tears streaming down her face, her freckles seem painted on her ashen face. Jace is holding her hand tightly.

The two snorkelers fall to the ground, utterly exhausted. The young woman is clinging to her boyfriend, sobbing uncontrollably. The young man is evidently in shock, mechanically shaking his head back and forth. This was certainly not what they imagined when they signed up for the Adventure of Your Life on Silfra Scuba's website. Barbu and Simi are also holding each other fast. Only now that they have spoken the fatal words, does what they said become real. Behind them, the water is churning yet they are encapsulated in deathly silence. Chuck is the first to move, the first to set aside the horrors witnessed in the name of survival. He gets to his feet with a moan, "We have to…" he presses out, but the Earth begins to tremble anew, and he comes no further.

An ear-splitting howl and staccato detonations wrench the Earth, tearing open a myriad of fissures. Pressurized water shoots up in sky-high fountains and all of them are thrown back down holding on to anything their fingers find on the ice-cold ground.

Thirty seconds later, it is quiet again as if a long dead and deeply buried giant has come back to life, wrestling to free himself from his stony crypt and is now gathering his strength for the final thrust. They wait, breath held, to see his massive form break through the asphalt, rising, roaring and squashing them like so many ants. The silence is terrifying.

Piet is the first one on his feet. As if molded from the rock he is standing on, he points at the edge of Silfra, his mouth opening and closing soundlessly. There, on the edge of Silfra, is Mickey standing on a boulder and waving wildly with both arms.

Ian charges up in street clothes, his face lobster red, mobile in hand, half barking, half gasping, "Get everyone to the parking lot and strip down. Toss everything out of the van. Help is on the way!" They all rise heavily to their feet, staring at Ian as if he's speaking Chinese. For a moment, no one moves or speaks. Then Chuck turns and races as fast he can toward the parking lot, without looking back. Simi, Barbu, Emma, Jace and the two tourists follow like iron chips after a magnet. Piet stumbles quickly in the other direction toward Silfra. "Not a trace of the four teams from other operators," Ian tells Sam. "Their vans are still standing on the parking lot."

The two men scramble over lava debris toward Piet. Sam chokes on his breath when he spots Mickey, not ten meters away from safety, precariously balanced on a crag rising in the center of a bottomless pit filled with seething water and belching steam fountains. Mickey is searching the waters beneath him, looking for Julia. When he catches Sam's eyes, he points below, his despair palpable. Sam signals him to try and climb over to shore, a hopeless enterprise. Mickey shakes his head, wheeling his arms to keep his balance. Then, to Sam's horror, he sees his friend begin to climb down the other side of the pinnacle. Sam turns desperately to the parking lot and then back to Mickey, but he has vanished from his line of vision. They can't just leave him there! But the gap between them might as well be an ocean. A rope! He thought if he had a rope, he could easily toss it the short distance. Do they have rope in the van? A thunderous rupture makes the question moot and Sam can only watch as the crag topples backward.

Gone. Sam is rooted to the spot, gaping into the broiling precipice. NO! His brain refuses to register what just happened. Right in front of his eyes. Paralyzed, Sam is an island of stunned silence amid the apocalypse. Just this morning, he saw Mickey and Julia at the breakfast table. Mickey laughing and Julia, one arm slung over his shoulder, shaking her head over one of his frequent, off-color jokes. That was just a few hours ago. Certainly, Mickey's just pulling his leg! Any second now, he will see Mickey and Julia's heads peeping over the ridge of rock and the laugh will be on Sam. In shock, he watches Piet sprinting toward the parking lot and Ian toward the lagoon. He is alone, unable to move.

Horns blast from the parking lot. Sam's brain kicks into overdrive and his body jerks in response. As if floodgates open, adrenaline shoots through his veins, his knees go soft and then he's flying from the rocks, his feet propelling the Earth's revolutions. In seconds, he is on the parking lot where Chuck, Piet, Jace, Emma, Barbu and Simi are gathered around the ranger's Land Rover, still in their dry suits.

"Ian's gone looking for the ranger. The two snorkelers took off in their car. They're still fully geared up! We have to get out of here!" Chuck's voice breaks. "NOW!"

Sam looks in the Land Rover. Marek, the ranger's husky, has gone feral with fear, barking hysterically and throwing himself against the window. Sam lays his hand on the glass and speaks soothingly in an attempt to calm him. He is good with dogs and is the only one among them who has pet and conversed with Marek. But Marek only howls in frustration, his wolfish snout pressed against the glass.

Once more, the Earth throws them off their feet. Sam, holding onto the car door, opens it and Marek is on him in a heartbeat. Standing over him, slaver dripping from his jaws, he barks and growls in Sam's face. Sam goes completely limp, offers his throat and is careful not to look in Marek's eyes. He catches Jace ready to step to his aid.

"Go away. Just keep out of his way," Sam warns between his teeth. Marek looks up and rockets off to Silfra in search of his mistress, his dog's heart filled with ferocious love. Bring the pack to safety.

"The key's in the ignition!" Chuck cries triumphantly. Sam scrambles to his feet and screams in Chuck's face, "We can't just leave them here – we have to find Ian and the ranger!"

"Look behind you!" Chuck shouts back and everyone turns to Langjökull. A brown river is rolling down the glacier, coming directly at them.

From where they stand, it seems to be moving in slow motion, yet they can see it displacing huge boulders or gobbling them up, incorporating them into the flood. The scraggy pines break like toothpicks as the unmuzzled snout tumbles down the slope toward the valley. As it spreads, its intense heat breaks off colossal blocks of ice that melt and add to the momentum, gravity urging it onwards. A lahar, shoots through Sam's mind, exactly what Jon described.

"WE HAVE TO GO NOW!" Chuck bellows, jumping into the driver's seat and revving the engine until it howls. At that moment, with a deafening roar the asphalt parking lot bursts open. They're trapped. The access road to Ring Road is gone. Seconds of shocked silence. Chuck revs the motor again and Piet and Jace rip open the back doors, taking Emma into their middle. Sam dives into the front seat and sees Barbu and Simi catapulting into the back. Doors slam shut. Simi screams in panic, "Go! Go! GO!"

Chuck spins the Land Rover's back wheels, pivoting the massive vehicle. Sam looks back to Silfra. Not a trace of Ian and the ranger.

Maddeningly slowly, Chuck maneuvers the Land Rover down the slope over lava boulders and mossy tundra floor. Miraculously, they are not struck from above. Twenty more meters and they will be on the access road and can floor it out of hell.

"Oh hurry, please," Barbu begs from the back, his face pressed against the side window. Emma is completely bent over, her nose between her legs, her hands clawing into Piet and Jace's flesh on either side.

Loud scraping vibrates through the chassis. Ignoring it, Chuck keeps going and they clear the last mound of petrified lava. Fat off-road wheels hit asphalt and Chuck stands on the gas pedal. The powerful motor wails, wheels spin and the car careens. Chuck, sweating, wrenches the steering wheel back and forth, taming the beast. No one makes a sound. They are one mind, fully focused on keeping the vehicle on the road and ahead of the encroaching fury. As they zoom past the Visitor's Center, the lahar rises to crush them. Slip-. rock, water mass and colossal blocks of ice. Rising hot magma penetrated the ancient glacier, melting it from the inside within seconds, triggering mighty explosions that severed massive ice blocks from the mother berg.

"Waaah!" everyone screams except Chuck who is bent over the steering wheel, teeth clamped, eyes manic, gas foot flat. The T-intersection is approaching. We'll never make the curve at this speed, Sam thinks and is tempted to close his eyes. But if this is his final moment, he wants to see it.

Nanoseconds ahead of the tsunami, he takes the curve, letting the Land Rover levitate sideways over the road. When the wheels reconnect with asphalt, the heavy jeep tips to the side and they're coasting on two wheels. Sam's head bangs hard against the window when all four tires smack back onto the road. He turns and sees Piet rubbing his forehead and Barbu surfaces from behind the back seat with blood spurting over his left eye.

Chuck gears down and charges on, engine roaring. Behind them, the terrain cuts a slice of the lahar and sends it thundering into Silfra. Sam says a silent goodbye to Ian, Marek and the ranger. The greater part of the torrent is still on their tail, declivities adding momentum. The plateau narrows as it approaches the coastline before dropping steeply down to Mosfellsbaer, a village alongside the coastal road to Reykjavik. The wave will gain pressure in the bottleneck, becoming a fatal injection plunging into the bay below.

"Faster! Faster!" Jace and Piet shriek. "It's catching up to us! Oh God!" A wall of ear-shattering sound drowns out their cries and the motor's howling. It looks like the wave is erecting itself behind them in slow motion, an immeasurable wall. Ice blocks as high as houses are thrown down in its path, only to be swallowed and absorbed as the wave surges forward. Jarred and tossed from side to side, Sam tries to observe the monster in the side mirror. Objects may appear closer than they are a decal on the mirror declares. Let's hope so! Sam's mouth twists into a humorless crooked grin. His senses are short-circuiting. It has always been like this. As a young man, he had earned extra money driving an ambulance, and the more serious and deadlier the situation, the less he could get his mouth into an appropriate position. It was like he was the hero in some horror film, trying to escape the encroaching demons. He watched through an invisible shield, protecting him, isolating him. Like now. When he couldn't cope, he grinned.

The jeep raced on, bucking and jumping rents and crevices in the road like a stampeding buffalo. Tremors and quakes have done their work. The springs bottom out each time the massive vehicle crashes back down on the asphalt after flying over quake-induced half-pipes, sending its passengers to the roof and back. Should a tire blow, they are doomed.

A toppled caravan lay on the roadside in front of them. A man in a yellow emergency vest stands waving wildly, a woman and two children beside him. Chuck pulls the Land Rover to the left and passes them up. Less than a second later, Sam watches in the mirror as the lahar devours them.

"We'll never make it," Jace bellows, "it's nearly on us!" Flying debris gleefully dents the roof and cracks the back window. Chuck gives no sign he hears. His eyes are glued to the rollercoaster rising and falling ahead; his right foot flat on the floor.

"Look up there on the right after the next turn. There's a gravel lane going up the mountain side, on top is a mobile antenna. I was there last winter. It's our only chance!" Jace yells from the back seat.

"Where?"

"About eighty meters ahead, but we'll never make it at this speed!"

Chuck grits his teeth. He can see it now, a gentle right curve. He can't slow down; the raging mass is less than eighty meters behind them. Wildly determined, he turns the wheel and lets the Land Rover drift over the road and onto the gravel lane. Bucking ferociously, Chuck's passengers scream in terror, but he's deaf and dumb.

Charged with adrenaline, he wrestles the car into position, and they begin to climb the steep slope to the red antenna at breakneck speed. Their very bones are rattled and jolted over the gravel, but the antenna is coming closer. It has to be at least fifty meters above the valley floor, and that should be enough.

Braking hard, the heavy off-road vehicle stops centimeters from the antenna's concrete plinth. They are immediately enveloped in a thick cloud of dust.

Ding, ding – ding, ding – ding, ding. Sam listens to his own fitful breathing, gasping in time with the dinging. Not one of them had thought to put on their seatbelt.

NINE

Y ESSS! You did it, you son of a gun!" Sam shouts, slapping Chuck on the back. " "Let's get out of here," and he throws open the door, inviting wallowing dust into the car and their lungs. Coughing and spluttering they exit the steaming, sighing vehicle and gather close, staring down at the devastation they escaped.

Not fifteen meters from where they stand, a fierce, determined flood thunders past and they hold onto one another to avoid being sucked up in the slipstream. Ice blocks the size of the Empire State Building surface and are swallowed, surface and are swallowed. Unidentifiable, mangled debris swept up in the wave's furious path bobs and sinks or is thrown wide. They lean as far from the deluge as possible. Terrifyingly close and absolutely lethal.

Gaping, the group of survivors are riveted to the scene. An apocalyptic landscape emerging before their very eyes in a matter of minutes. Sam points to Langjökull. A column of black-brown smoke rockets high into the sky, raining fire. Dull explosions eject gigantic, glowing boulders over several kilometer's trajectory. The volcano is aroused, death and destruction its bedmates.

The Earth trembles and shifts slightly beneath their diving boots. Instinctively, they fall back to the car, their most recent refuge and savior. Only Chuck and Sam are hypnotized by the water masses eating into their mountain slope, stealing layer by layer and carrying them away. The hungry beast will be fed.

"On the plinth, NOW!" Sam roars.

Chuck is the first one up and Sam heaves and shoves his colleagues up to safety one after the other before Piet and Chuck grab his wrists and pull him up onto the plinth. The ground shudders, and a quake knocks them off their feet. They hold tight to each other's hands. Vibrating, crunching, cracking. The lava boulder below them tears, opening deep crevices. Metal crunching, the Land Rover slides backward into a fissure, its fall stopped by the front wheels, giving the impression it is holding on for dear life. Suddenly, all goes quiet. Even the rolling wave has diminished by half. Water, ice and debris flow past. Have they survived?

"Look!" Jace bursts into the silence, pointing into one of the fissures. Whitish pebbles shine from a hollow in the black stone. Jace jumps down from the plinth.

"What do you want with them, you idiot?" Sam calls after him. Jace seems to have lost his mind.

"Those are raw diamonds, you idiot yourself! I know what they look like, my cousin is a diamond dealer. I'm sure they're diamonds!" Jace calls back enchanted.

Sam watches Emma, Barbu, Simi, Piet and finally Chuck climb down to Jace. Sam cannot believe what he's seeing. We scrape by with our lives, lose friends not ten minutes ago, and now we've hit it rich? Sam is gob-smacked by it all. Shaking his head, he climbs down and joins the others in the fissure.

"Take only the milky-white stones," Jace instructs, and they begin stuffing pebble and potato-sized stones into the pockets on the legs of their diving suits.

Jace's discovery is the perfect lifesaver for their overtaxed minds; a welcome distraction, transmuting pain, loss and terror onto crevices filled with sudden wealth. As if out at sea, in the midst of a gale, the captain turns the sails and they fly in a wholly new direction. The flipside of paralyzing

helplessness in the face of natural disaster is ec-
stasy at the prospect of untold riches. They now
are no longer concerned with their survival since
they have, thus far, survived. A switch so utterly di-
chotomous, so all-consuming, any rational thought
is swept away before it can begin to form.

"We're rich, rich, rich!" Simi sings coarsely, en-
raptured. Sam stands and watches before he, too,
kneels down and begins to collect the precious
stones. What the hell are we doing? he asks himself yet continues to fill his pockets.

"There's more! Look! Huge ones!" Simi exclaims and points to another fissure somewhat
lower. Before anyone can say anything, he jumps
down to a shelf and triumphantly raises a white
stone the size of a softball into the air.

"Come away from there right now!" Sam commands. The rent is less than a meter from a deep
gorge filled with rushing, most likely toxic water.
Simi grins and rolls his find to the jeep's back
wheel above. That was all it took. The ledge upon
which the jeep's front wheels were resting begins
to crumble and slide downwards. Simi jumps up
and catches hold of the rear axle, his legs dan-
gling over the ravaging river below. Chuck and

Barbu run up and throw their bodies onto the car's hood, hoping to lever Simi out of the fissure. Sam and Jace each wrap themselves around a man's legs. The jeep is perilously close to the edge and the Earth beneath grinding to powder.

"Take my hand brother," Barbu hollers and stretches his arm below. Simi is hanging onto the axle with one hand and onto his white stone with the other.

"What are you doing dammit! Drop the fucking thing! Quick!" Barbu shouts at his brother.

"That's the biggest diamond ever found – take it! Take it!" Simi calls back. Barbu tries to grasp the swaying stone without taking his weight from the hood, but Chuck pushes him away and stretches his body toward Simi. The diamond falls over Simi into the deep and instead of taking Chuck's hand, Simi follows the stone with his eyes.

Chuck grabs Simi's wrist just as the jeep slips over the rim. For a split second the two men look into one another's eyes. Chuck has no choice, he lets go and clamps onto Barbu to keep from falling, too. The heavy vehicle follows forces not human. Barbu and Chuck, their legs held by Jace and Sam, slam down on the edge of the precipice. They see the car pirouette and delicately lay itself over Simi. With a mighty splash, the two-ton vehicle bombs into the water, vanishing in a trice, with Simi somewhere beneath. It is over in the blink of an eye. No pain, not even enough time to absorb what is happening to him. Just Chuck's eyes on his, then darkness.

An inhuman howl from a deeply damaged creature rents the air. "Siiiimmmmiiii!" Barbu keens, glaring into the deeps.

Chuck grabs hold from beneath Barbu. They are laying on the sharp edge and Chuck feels a searing pain in his ribcage. Jace and Sam kept them from going over the edge, but as the hood slipped from them they crashed hard on the splintered ground, Chuck underneath, with Barbu's weight intensifying the impact. The pain is drilling into his brain, taking his breath away. Chuck retreats to a tiny, coherent space in his mind, drawing strength from his indomitable survival instinct. Do not let go, do not let go, do not let go, his inner voice chants insistently.

Jace and Sam are on their bellies, their arms clamped onto their friends' legs. Emma and Piet climb down to them, managing to pull them up onto the remaining narrow ridge below the antenna plinth.

"We have to get up there," Chuck gasps, indicating the antenna plinth. Pooling their strength, they manage to help each other scramble up until all of them are on the plinth again. With every breath, Chuck feels a piercing pain in his chest. He must have broken a rib or two. It hurts like hell. Barbu's equally piercing pain is of another sort. He gazes into the abyss, his face slack with shock.

"Oh my God," Emma whispers, one hand over her mouth, the other holding onto the antenna, "look at that."

Rising slowly, like very old people, they turn and look out at the bay. Chuck, held upright with Sam's shoulder to lean on, gasps, "What the fuck!"

A tidal wave. The towering ice blocks tumbling through the lahar's water masses and scree has wiped out every human, horse and homestead on the plateau, steamrolled over the village Mosfellsbaer and crashed into the ocean. Now, huge waves are gathering and returning to deluge Reykjavik. Force and counterforce, natural laws. Two islands, Videy and Engey, form a bottleneck into the bay, giving the wave an opportunity to break and distribute its power.

They are a good twenty kilometers from the city, enveloped in dust, but Reykjavik is flooded in brilliant sunlight. Despite the distance, they clearly hear the thundering impact of water on solid. They watch as the tidal wave swallows the beach promenade, smashes against the hill, completely veiling Hallgrímskirkja Cathedral in huge clouds of spume. The vision will haunt them for the rest of their lives.

Minutes pass as they witness the ravenous sea thresh, harvest and gobble up homes.

Emma sobs in Jace's arms. Barbu stares hypnotized at the continuing flow of water and mud in the abyss at their feet.

Simi. Just this morning they had shared Romanian jokes over breakfast. They had calculated their savings and wondered if it was enough to repair the family homestead in the Carpathian Mountains. Had played out scenarios of starting their own families on ancient family ground. The prospect of immeasurable wealth wiped the past and future from Simi's consciousness. Too many shocks in too short a time and he even forgot his own life.

They had never had enough, had grown up with hunger and want. Constant need shapes a person. As a child, it is just the way things are. Hunger is normal, cold is normal, that's life. But while learning more of the world, anger ferments and a human being comes to a fork in the road. One turn leads to resignation, the other to hope. Miracles do happen. For a few moments in his short life, Simi had held the miracle in his hand.

Barbu searches for a place in his mind where none of this has happened; a painless place, quieting his immeasurable loss. He sinks to the ground, drawing his knees to his chest and burying his face in his hands. He wishes he could turn off the world, but of course he can't. His tears flow soundlessly, forming rivulets of grief and bewilderment. There is little outer sign of his weeping and pain, but Sam kneels down beside him, mechanically stroking his back. He has no words of comfort; he can only offer his presence and shoulder his share of grief.

Piet unzips Chuck's diving suit. Chuck is on the ground, moaning and heaving. "Bloody hell!" he spits out, "We're alive! At least for now."

Piet sweeps his fingers over Chuck's chest. Chuck cries out in pain when his fingers touch the lowest right rib. "Just as I thought," said Piet. "One of your ribs is broken or crushed. Highly painful, but not life threatening." Chuck rolls his eyes and pulls the zipper up with an aggravated jerk.

Still kneeling by Barbu, Sam turns to Langjökull. Where is Marie right now? Will he ever see her again? Everything – everything – has changed in less than an hour. An excruciating uncertainty takes hold of him, burning torturously. They have watched their colleagues die. They have seen tourists, their customers out for a bit of adventure, devoured by Iceland's force majeure, the creators of her very existence – ice and fire. What now? Are those raw diamonds or is this collective insanity? If they really are diamonds, then they are rich, unbe-lievably rich. Is that a blessing amid disaster or the beginning of the real catastrophe? Sam wishes he knew.

TEN

Grieving, depleted, and their pockets full of possibly precious stones, they begin the laborious trek to Reykjavik over the plateau's lava fields. With Sam supporting Chuck, the two take the lead, picking out a path between riven, razor-sharp lava boulders. The keen stones have long notched and punctured the soles of their diving suits. Thick as they may be, they are made for short walks before divers put on their flippers. Not for twenty-kilometer hikes over rugged terrain.

Looking down from the final rise before the descent toward the bay, they see the Ring Road. Aside from a gaping hole denoting the tidal wave's path, it seems to be intact along the few kilometers to V18. Beyond, where the city should be, orange and blue lights are pulsating through a thick veil of ash as finely ground as confectioner's flour. Endless summer daylight has been dimmed to an eternal twilight. A revolting taste of sulfurous ash coats their mouths, is lodged between their teeth. Eyes bloodshot; throats congested. The scene below could be straight out of a disaster movie, an end-of-the-world scenario, were it not for one exception. This is real. No one will wake up, relieved to find it was all a bad dream. Nor would they walk out into summer night air, untouched and entertained.

Although the failing light allows only an idea of the damage done, the city has been hard hit. The houses lining the bay are no more. Gone. Emma collapses on a boulder, buries her face in her hands and cries bitterly. Jace kneels before her, offering solace he doesn't possess. Not even Chuck has a word to say. His weight supported by Piet now, they view the devastation below silently. They must keep going. Resting only intensifies their thirst and no one knows if the ash is toxic. They must find drinking water and clothes. None of them are hungry. Sam pulls Emma up wordlessly and clasps her tightly in his arms. He looks in her eyes and nods several times. Somehow, everything will be all right. He begins to walk with his arm around her and she allows herself to be led.

Finally, they reach the road and progress more quickly. It had taken them endless hours to cross the precarious lava fields. The stones in their pockets click and clack, rubbing against their skin through the neoprene, reminding them of their presence with every step. Here we are, your carefree future, your endless possibilities – keep going and put this madness behind you!

Early the next morning they limp over the roundabout, turning off where they assume the access road to V18 to be. Mud flats littered with containers from the harbor stretch over the entire slope to the turnpike. It is if a giant child has dumped out his Lego collection, some of them twenty meters long and weighing several tons. Many have been lifted and tossed like so many pebbles against houses, smashing walls and windows or hurled high only to fall and flatten roofs.

Up on the turnpike fire engines and ambulances struggle to make headway through the slick sediment and wreckage. Their massive tires, a godsend in rugged terrain, are repeatedly defeated by the size and density of debris. Thick black smoke rises from several places further ahead in the city. You would think with all that water, nothing could burn. Yet the force of wreckage, boulders and ice blocks flung far and wide demolished gas mains and shredded electric cables. Reykjavik's infrastructure, its lifeline to the world, has been laid waste.

V18 is deserted. Crackling cables and steaming water pipes hang in the air like torn arteries from what was once the building's left wing. The right wing, including their living quarters, is still intact.

Amazing luck. Stairs and kitchen can be seen through the gaping hole. Sam and Jace run up while Barbu, Piet and Emma tend to Chuck, who collapses gasping on the bottom step.

Barbu sits heavily next to Chuck, his face in his hands. His shoulders shake slightly, but his weeping is as soundless as his brother's grave. Chuck gives him a sidelong glance, painfully lifts his left arm and lays it over Barbu's shoulders. It is the only gesture of comfort he knows, having been told by his drill sergeant that it was the proper thing to do when a friend died in combat. Like bandaging a broken nose, this was the right treatment for a broken heart.

"Where are they?" Jace wonders. "There had to be at least thirty people here when the earthquake struck."

Sam shakes his head. Door by door, they check all the rooms for some sign of life. By the look of things, they had left in a great hurry.

"They either fled or were evacuated," Sam concludes, rubbing his bald head.

"But where to?"

"There must be a gathering place. We'll just follow the ambulances; they will take us to wherever people are. Let's get out of here!"

"Wait a second, we should collect some things we might need, and first of all get out of these suits!"

"Yes, let's," Sam agrees, but instead of heading for his room, pulls out his cellphone. He thinks about what last night should have been. Marie, where are you? He stumbles around the kitchen, his arm stretched out, looking for reception. There! Vodaphone, one bar. With shaking fingers, he opens his bookmarked numbers and taps on Marie. Sam's breathing becomes ragged, his heart is pounding. He presses one finger against his left ear and the filthy mobile to his right. After three rings, Marie answers.

"Sam? – C'est toi? You are alive!?" Then, crackling and white noise, interspersed with holes of dead silence. Sam jumps up on a chair, holding his cellphone in the air, the connection is still live.

"Marie! My God, where are you?" he shouts at his phone and presses it back to his ear.

Jace, Emma and Piet are standing at the kitchen door, gazing at him with rapt attention. Barbu, supporting Chuck slowly comes up behind them. Sam gives them a wave and needlessly puts his finger to his lips. They are silent and waiting.

He has reached Marie and dances precariously on the chair to hold the connection.

"We are...krrsss...ffttrrtp...trrr...dral and you? Who is with...rrrtsss...brrr...krrrttt?"

"Emma, Jace, Barbu, Piet and Chuck are here with me at V18! Are you at the cathedral? Who is with you?" Sam shouts back.

"s... krsttkrts...frrt...are.... rrkkrt – tut-tut-tut"

"Marie, my darling, I'm coming to get you! I am so happy to hear your voice! I love you!" Sam yells at the mobile, even though he knows the connection has been broken.

"Well, well, that's news," Chuck is grinning from ear to ear. His chortling is abruptly cut off by painful coughing he attempts to repress.

Sam is still standing on the chair, his arm stretched out, a post-modern statue his friends admire in obvious amusement. It's good to have something to smile about. Sam stares at his cell phone. He may have lost the connection, but it appears there are still some antenna masts with an independent power source. That's excellent news!

He jumps down from the chair and points to his cellphone, "Marie! I believe she said they were gathered at the Hallgrímskirkja. That makes sense, the cathedral is high enough to have been spared the wave. That's where we should head now. But first, let's get changed into some warm clothes."

But Chuck, leaning against the door as Barbu has slipped away, first wants to know, "How long have you two been an item?"

"What does that matter now? We know where the others are," Emma interjects while Jace and Piet simply stare at Sam in amazement.

Barbu comes back. He's changed into sturdy clothes, his backpack filled and ready to go. "We know where we need to go, so get ready," he commands tersely. His face is lined with grief, yet he is the one to keep calm and prepare for the next step they need to take.

They scatter down the hallways. It is an enormous stroke of luck that their side of the building has been more or less left unscathed. They change and pack whatever they think is necessary – and what wasn't lost at Þingvallavatn. Emma goes with Chuck and wraps a support bandage around his ribcage. He immediately feels better. Although breathing is still painful, it is a manageable pain. The man is made of iron.

They gather back in the kitchen, warmly dressed and Chuck places a small, empty backpack on the table. "I suggest we put all the stones in here."

"Isn't that a bit risky?" Piet objects. "If we lose the backpack, we lose them all."

"All for one and one for all," Chuck grins and empties his pockets into the backpack. The others follow suit.

While Barbu was waiting, he had scrounged together the sparse forgotten foodstuffs, bread, butter, crackers and some cheese and placed them on the table along with two bottles of water. They haven't eaten or drank since yesterday morning. They share equally and munch mechanically in silence, passing the bottles from hand to hand. Finally, they all look at the small pack of stones on the table. Sam picks it up and looks each of them in the eyes. They nod, and he slings it over his shoulder.

When they are standing on the turnpike, Jace points toward downtown Reykjavik. The cathedral is a bit over two kilometers away. A short distance down the turnpike is a direct lane winding up to Hallgrímskirkja. Before them is a huge expanse of wreckage. Weary as they are, they will have to navigate it somehow.

After an hour's march, scrambling over, crawl-
ing under and threading through upturned, mangled cars and containers, smashed concrete, endless rocks and boulders and common household
items such as toasters and children's toys, they
reach the turn off to Hallgrímskirkja. They have not
seen a single human being. Their eyes following
the road in front of them, they silently gaze at
what is left of the once picture-perfect city. Only
an atom bomb could have wreaked more havoc
than Nature's wrath. Old wooden houses have
been swept away, piled up in huge heaps of
cracked beams and splintered glass. Only the
larger concrete houses remain standing, their windows burst, dead eyes staring. The Harpa Opera
House, once an architectural artwork of glass and
steel standing at the harbor like a glittering iceberg, has been rammed with ships from the harbor, its roof hanging bent over the plaza, its in-
nards spewing flames. Black smoke rises lazily into
the ash-laden air.

Barbu found his camera in V18 and is taking
photos of the mass destruction, freezing the sight
for a time when he could better cope with it. Sam
and Barbu have often hiked together over the
neighboring lava fields, Barbu with camera at
hand. He is a talented photographer and Sam was
impressed with Barbu's knack for capturing a

meaningful ambient on film. What emotions will these pictures trigger in viewers around the world? The photos will make him famous. As if reading his thoughts, Barbu turns to Sam, "They are only for me. I want to remember the hell we endured."

"We're still in the middle of it," Piet reminds him, pointing to the lane going up the hill.

But the going is easier than they at first feared it would be. There was little rubble here, the wave having spent itself on the city. Arriving at the top, they finally find people. Deep relief cascades through them. Since yesterday, they have all harbored a subconscious fear – are we the only ones left alive? Rescue teams have erected an emergency center on the spacious plaza in front of the cathedral. Makeshift tents surround an antenna reaching high into the sky. Jeeps, fire engines and ambulances are arriving from the other side of the hill, their blinking lights sweeping over the assembly. No sirens, no loud chatter. A heavy, dull near silence, broken only by an occasional call in Icelandic. People are milling around, some purposefully, some defeated.

The statue of Leifur Eriksson, the man who allegedly discovered the American continent around 1000 A.D., centuries before Columbus, did not survive the earthquake. The bronze sculpture has fallen from its pedestal, smashed to the ground and broken in two. Rescue teams mounted the antenna on his concrete plinth.

Ghostly silence and concentrated activity pervade the scene. As if they are carrying out an emergency drill amid clouds of ash. But where are all the people? These few cannot possibly be the only survivors of a two-hundred-thousand-soul area!

Chuck enters the tent next to the antenna and addresses an Icelander. The fireman tries to wave him away, but Chuck is not an easy man to brush off.

"Wounded are in the cathedral," the man reports brusquely. "Anyone who can walk is being brought to Keflavik. Busses are waiting next to the domestic airport; the road seems to be intact – we'll all get away."

"Keflavik? What's the use in going there?" Piet interjects, shaking his head. "The airport is definitely closed; no machine can fly in this ash."

Emma agrees, "Exactly. We'll only be stranded there, hoping a ship will make it through to pick us up."

"Well, I'm going there," Chuck informs them. "I need to find Seydür. You all can stay here if you want."

Sam empathizes. Not so many weeks ago, Chuck fell in love with a pretty Icelander. And he fell hard. Since then, he's made a complete turna-round. This notorious womanizer; the guy stalking every cute tourist like all the others, was tamed overnight. When he wasn't in the city with Seydür, he stayed at V18, playing cards with the others. If Sam thought Marie is in Keflavik, he would be rac-ing with Chuck to get to the bus.

"Okay. Good luck my friend and take good care of yourself!" Sam says and gives him a not-too-tight hug.

"I'll be back!" Chuck laughs his horse laugh, "so don't think you'll be getting away with my share of the loot!" he says, carefully hugging each of them before limping off to catch a bus.

While the others scatter in search of something to eat and fresh water, Sam walks to the cathedral. Above him, he sees people looking out the win-dows of the broad pyramidal church spire. Enter-ing the nave, his breath catches in his throat. Pews are stacked high on the side. From the entrance with its majestic organ to the far end where the altar stands, people are laying on the floor. The only sounds are an occasional moan, otherwise it is oppressively quiet. Some people are moving around, tending to the injured. Dim light falls through the large, plain glass side windows. The cathedral's defiant architecture has evidently weathered the disaster without damage. It's been hours since the last tremor, but Sam is certain there is more to come.

Slowly turning and scanning the room, he sees Marie near the staircase to the tower. She has her back to him, and it appears she is tending to someone. Sam threads his way between the wounded and when he is close enough, he sees she is standing next to Ilias. Ilias is dead. His face is filthy, his mouth is open, and his dead eyes view the ceiling through half-closed lids.

Sam touches Marie gently on her shoulder and she cringes violently, whirls around and stares at him for several seconds without recognition. She seems to doubt her eyes. Sam softly says her name and she comes to life, falling into his arms, burying her face in his shoulder.

"Mon Dieu – Sam!" She says between sobs again and again. Sam tries to soothe her. He takes her head firmly in his hands and looks into her eyes.

"Marie, you can't imagine how glad I am to have found you! You're alive! Tell me, are you okay? Where is everyone from V18?"

"Oh Sam! You're alive! Incroyable! I am so happy to see you! We heard that no one made it out of Þingvellir alive. How can that be, that you are here? Are you alone? How did you get away?"

"Later, cheríe – Piet, Jace, Emma, Chuck and Barbu are with me, we made it out together."

"No one else?"

Sam shakes his head and Marie looks at him aghast. She holds her hand before her mouth and tries to grasp the ungraspable. Ilias is the first person she has seen from V18 and only six people made it out of Silfra alive. She has had incredible luck. She was in the city and ran into Jon who was beside himself. He was certain Katla was going to erupt any moment and he must warn the people. But the authorities have blocked his cellphone and website. He would not stand for it; he has to let them know!

He pressed her to come with him, insisted on it. His demanding persistence frightened her, so she went along with him and he took her to the cathedral. The moment they arrived, the Earth began to tremble. She wanted to get to V18, but Jon held her there, promising the massive cathedral is the only place she would be truly safe. And he was right. From the cathedral balcony she saw the cloud of ash erupt over Þingvellir and watched in horror as the monumental mass of mud, ice, water and stone plowed into the bay, pushing the waters back only to have them return in force and crash over Reykjavik. The sound was ear-shattering and clouds of spume rose as high as the cathedral. She heard houses crack and splinter, the whine of bursting steel. She saw ships and containers heaved out of the harbor, flying high and landing with deafening crashes, flattening everything in their path. And then, it was over. Amid the hissing, blubbering water she heard the cries of human beings calling for help, for their friends, for their families. Their voices faint like invisible songbirds calling from varying points in a vast wooded park. An unspeakable, heart-wrenching soundtrack to the destruction laid out before her. Soon after, the first people arrived, filthy and limping, carrying wounded on their backs, supporting one another. Only then did the sirens go off. The city wailed like a wounded moose, inconsolably keening. There had been no warning. No escape. Police and fire department rescue vehicles rolled onto the plaza.

A gathering of giant trucks with massive tires for Iceland's craggy terrain. The emergency center was established; helpers coordinated. A hopeless enterprise. Too much of the infrastructure had been demolished, allowing only sketchy communication. Survivors must be treated and evacuated. Anyone buried alive would stay that way. Save who could be saved.

Marie helped other unscathed survivors clear the nave to make room for the wounded. She was among a pitiful handful of spared human wholeness. Of the thousands living in Reykjavik, only a few hundred survived or found safety elsewhere.

"We have to go, Marie. I'm afraid things are going to only get worse," Sam urges Marie, her head still held in his hands.

She nods, "They are bringing everyone to Keflavik for evacuation. The busses are waiting behind the hill. Evidently, the roads are intact."

"We don't know that for certain, Marie. It could be that they all will get trapped on the way to the airport. And if they don't...well, I can't imagine any aircraft starting or landing in this ash-rain."

"But where do you suggest we go, Sam? Are we going to die here?" Marie asks matter-of-factly, drawing strength from the need to act. Sam's aliveness reminds her of her own, and a fatalistic calm takes hold. She is ready to guide or be guided.

Sam takes her by the hand. They climb the steps to the tower where they encounter Jon at the top. He has hauled up a car battery, his laptop and a compact satellite dish in his backpack. He lays out the equipment on the balcony balustrade.

In answer to Sam's questioning look, he says, "These are souvenirs from the days before Iceland had blanket internet reception. I was traveling the island back then, collecting data from the gaging stations I was permitted to access. I wanted to write my own blog on volcanos and earthquakes. Good thing I held on to them. The MET network is still running and it's not good news!"

"Look, there!" he waves them over. "Aside from the earthquake and Langjökull's eruption, it seems that Katla is fully aroused, she's trembling and quaking impatiently."

"Yes," Sam says, "we noticed that in Vik."

"No, no, this is something completely different, Sam. Look at this tremor. That is magma rising and pushing outward, lifting stone and expanding the crater beneath the massive ice carapace. This is phenomenal!" Jon gasps in excitement.

Sam bends over the balustrade and peers over to the airport directly behind and below the cathedral on the coast. It looks like everything's still in one piece there, including the surrounding industrial area and the airport itself. Below, busses surrounded by orange blinking police cars swallow the meager converging groups of survivors. He could count them on two hands. Apparently, everything behind the crest was spared the tidal wave, but not the earthquake.

"Do you have binoculars?" Sam asks Jon, who promptly pulls them from his backpack and hands them to Sam.

A private jet is standing on the runway, a sleek, silver Gulfstream. Sam discovers a small Brazilian flag on the tailfin. Bruna!

"I know how we're going to get out of here," he remarks to Marie, giving her an abridged version of Bruna, her fiancé and the jet.

"Let's get the others and make a run for it. Jon, pack your stuff," he commands.

"Go? Are you crazy? This is the story of a lifetime! The MET only publishes status reports. They don't say a word about the true state of things. They don't mention Katla at all, issuing no warnings on the impact she might have. This is my big chance! I'll get my name all over the place in international media!" Jon protests vehemently.

"And what good will it do you when you're dead?" Marie asks, placing her hand on his shoulder.

Jon wipes her hand away and turns back to his data. Sam and Marie exchange a look and turn away without another word.

Back on the cathedral plaza, they look for the others. They find them clustered together at the commando tent and see Piet waving his arms emphatically, trying to convince the uniformed man of something. When Marie spots them, she releases a sharp cry that catches Piet's ear. He lowers his arms and whirls around. All the others turn toward Marie, too, who is running toward them jumping up to hug them all at once. They all laugh and cry at the same time, astonished and relieved to find familiar faces, alive and well, among the trickle of wounded and dying. They have survived, they have lived to see each other again while countless others are dead or missing.

Marie turns her tear-streaked face to Sam and before she can ask, he says, "Yes, Chuck was here, too. He took one of the busses to Keflavik in search of his darling Seydür."

Marie nods and smiles through her unceasing tears, "You have no idea how happy I am to see you. It's a miracle. I was certain no one could survive what happened at Þingvellir."

"Bad weeds grow tall," Piet remarks and immediately wishes he hadn't. He goes to Barbu and apologizes by placing his brow on Barbu's chest.

They sit on boulders in a circle and before Marie can begin to ask the thousand questions in her mind, Sam raises his hand, palm outwards, asking for her patience. He tells them of his plan to escape with Bruna in her jet. As expected, they are all raring to go. Get out of Dodge, so to speak, but not via Keflavik, the chances of getting stuck there are too great. Sam's plan is perfect, but they have to get going right away if they don't want to miss Bruna.

They set out immediately. The road down to the airport is eerily quiet. Aside from brick shards and other small debris scattered in yards and isolated cracks in the asphalt, there is little damage. As if the end-of-the-world destruction on the other side of the ridge had been a horror-trip hallucination. At the crossroads before turning into the airport, they see an elderly lady clearing debris from the orderly garden in front of her dapper wooden house. She is the first living being they have encountered beyond the cathedral. The old woman goes about her task with calm routine, obviously having survived any number of earthquakes. But does she have any idea of what might come? Barbu shoots Sam a questioning look, which Sam answers with a delicate bow of the head, raising his hands in a helpless gesture. Barbu nods, pressing his lips into a grim slit.

Just as they have all cleared the fence to the taxiway, the jet's engines come to life. Sam begins to run, gesticulating wildly, hoping the pilot will see him. But jets don't have rearview mirrors. And even if they had, the pilot is not about to get up, go to the cabin and politely ask Bruna if she is acquainted with the lunatics blocking his path.

Sam comes to a halt panting as the jet turns from the taxiway onto the runway. A short stop, and the engines erupt in a deafening roar. Then the machine begins to roll. Sam throws himself to the ground to avoid the jet blast. The plane rises and curves elegantly to the left before making a steep upward dive for the clouds.

"NO!" Sam bellows, "What the HELL are you doing, you idiot!" Evidently, the pilot thinks he can break through the ash clouds and fly above them. Doesn't the fool know what those tiny, razor-sharp ash particles are going to do to his machine? First, they will sand his windows opaque, so he is flying blind and then they will sandblast his engine blades to dust. I wish you luck, Bruna, he sends a heartfelt atheist's prayer. He sees the red back-lights blinking before the jet vanishes in the dense clouds of smoke and ash.

Sam rejoins his friends at the control tower. The place is deserted.

"And now?" Jace asks in general.

"We can still get one of the busses. What do you think?" Marie suggests.

Sam follows Piet and Barbu's gaze. To the right of the hangar is a Cessna 402, an eighties model famous for its unflinching reliability. Safety collars are hanging from the plane's rump, indicating it's ready to fly. There are six of them and six seats in the Cessna. But can he fly it? True, he did once have a private pilot's license, but only for visual flights with single-engine machines.

Emma is reading his mind, "Do you think you can fly it?"

"Well, I did have a license, but only for single-engine planes," Sam replies, still mustering the Cessna.

"But where will we fly to?" Marie interjects.

"To the Faroe Islands, about eight hundred kilometers southeast of Reykjavik," Piet answers for Sam. "But will the plane make it?" He adds, also scanning the machine.

"We have the wind in our favor and if the tank is full, we can make it. We'll need to fly close to the water's surface until we have cleared the ash clouds, but it could work. The only hitch is getting the crate into the air and, even trickier, getting us safe on the ground again," Sam muses.

"Then let's find out if the tank is full," Barbu suggests and the four men turn as one body.

"Are they completely déjanté? Crazy?" Marie turns to Emma, watching the men inspect the Cessna. Sam gets into the cockpit. "We can't just hijack an airplane! Especially not with a clueless pilot!"

"Yes, it's risky," Emma agrees, making to join the others, "but if Jon is right, we could easily die here. And flying with a clueless pilot looks like good alternative right now." Marie follows her reluctantly, shaking her head. Yet, she doesn't give a second thought to staying here, either. Not without Sam.

ELEVEN

"The tank is full, and the old girl seems to be ready for takeoff – all aboard!" Sam calls from the cockpit. He swings out of the door and walks around the machine removing all the safety collars.

The Cessna has eight seats and without luggage, the load is light. Sam takes a look around when everyone's buckled in. Jace and Emma are in the rearmost seats. Jace lifts the backpack with the stones. Good. Two empty rows and then Marie, directly behind him and Barbu next to her. Piet is in the co-pilot's seat. Very good, their weight is well-distributed. Now, what to do and which order? Sam searches his memory. First, turn the key to activate Avionics. The dashboard lights up – GPS, gyrocompass, radio direction finder, radio. Second, start the engines.

Sam pushes the ignition for the left engine. After a cough or two, the propellers begin to spin. He pushes the pedals to the floor to keep the machine from rolling. Now the second engine. Yes! The lady is over forty years old and you can still count on her, Sam thinks with a grin.

He carefully sets the plane in motion and heads for the runway. He checks the flaps with the yoke.

Light side wind coming off the sea, a welcome stroke of luck. Piet rolls his eyes at Sam's weaving approach to the liftoff point. He waves the checklist he finds in the side pocket.

"Not so easy after all this time, and then with two engines. Cross your fingers," Sam murmurs to himself. Piet reads out the checklist. Sam doesn't know what half of them refer to or where to find them when he does. He finds the altimeter, compass and tachometer, that will have to do. On the right is the switch for landing flaps and directly below it the one to retract the landing gear. What more can a man want?

"Please fasten your seatbelts and refrain from using the toilets. When we reach our cruising altitude, lunch will be served," he announces into the microphone, earning himself a slap on the neck from Marie. He tunes the radio to an emergency frequency. The airport on the Faroe Islands will certainly have all channels open, alert to incoming aircraft and Sam doesn't want to block any true emergencies. For the moment, they're fine. That should serve their purposes underway and when landing. Hopefully, Piet will find a map or reception on his cellphone to pinpoint the airport's location.

Sam takes a deep breath and while slowly and steadily exhaling through nearly closed lips, he gently pushes the yoke forward. The engines howl, the plane shudders. Sam is still holding back her thrust. He hasn't the foggiest how much of a running start she needs to liftoff, but the small green mark on the tach tells him he can begin to lift her snout at sixty-five knots. He opens his body's senses where memory is best stored. He lets the Cessna shake and rattle before abruptly releasing the brake. The plane rockets forward, eliciting a small shriek from Marie. The faster they go, the easier it is for Sam to hold her in the center of the runway. The rudder is doing its job and he can compensate the side wind surprisingly well. Now, at sixty-five knots and with an agitated sea marking the end of the runway in sight, he slowly pulls the yoke toward his chest.

The Cessna is airborne, and he takes the flaps in a notch. Immediately, a warning signal blares. He's too slow! Okay, easy does it, nose down a touch, flaps out again. He took them in too soon, but the Cessna's happy now and continues her ascent.

Not quite a hundred meters over the ocean, Sam levels out and switches the flaps into cruising position. Yup, that's right! he thinks to himself,

Iceland the windiest inhabited country on Earth! Their airship is tossed, thrown sideways and capers wildly over air pockets, but he manages to keep a relatively steady course along the Icelandic coastline, flying pretty much exactly between the ocean and ash clouds. They will have one last chance to land on the island's southeast tip. After that, it's open sea until Faroe Islands. Piet gives Sam a pat on the shoulder and raises his hand with the diver's okay sign for those in the back. Everyone responds with the same signal, thumb and forefinger in an 'O,' the other three fingers pointing upwards.

"Mon Dieu! Look!" Marie screams, pointing out the window. Down on their left, behind the village of Vik, a thick column of ash vomits violently into the already ash-covered sky. Katla! Way overdue, according to Jon and making up for lost time. They hear an earth-shaking roar over the Cessna's engines before they are hit by the shock wave, sending them spiraling downwards and all Sam sees is the ocean's surface rising to engulf them. He blocks out the panicking cries behind him and pulls with all his might, leveling the machine twenty meters before impact. Only now they are skimming like a tossed stone over broiling waves reaching for their underbelly while being bombarded from above. Katla is hurling red-hot stones hell-bent for leather high into the sky, heedless of where they fell. Although the black cloud of smoke is wafting northward, the wind has no influence on the sheer weighted mass of pitching fiery rock. If they are struck by even one small projectile, their flight and lives would end then and there. Sweat, terror and instinct converge on Sam's mind and body. He is not ready to die! A mere hundred meters ahead, a huge chunk of fluid magma hurtles past the plane, diving-bombing into the ocean and raising hot spume. Monstrous heat penetrates the Cessna. The Earth has declared war on Iceland. Jon has his story now.

Sam yanks the machine sharply to the right, sinking dangerously close to the waves. He pushes the yoke as far forward as possible. Full speed – cut and run!

The Cessna shoots off at less than fifteen meters over the sea. Glowing stones and boulders race past, splashing into the water far ahead of them, raising clouds of spume. Every second they are not struck is another second closer to escape. We have to make it, Sam thinks, gritting his teeth. I want to live! He casts a glance behind him. Marie, Emma and Jace are bent double, their heads on their knees, as if expecting impact any moment. Only Barbu is gazing serenely out the window. Iceland is behind them. Only twenty-four hours ago they were preparing tours, chattering on about tourists, money, politics and food. They acted as if their lives would go on this way forever. Guides, tourists, love. Sam looks over to Piet who is tapping his cellphone. Piet returns the glance and shakes his head, "No reception! Your GPS is also out!" he shouts over the intercom and draws the map onto his knees.

Sam looks at this compass spinning from side to side. There must be iron particles in the smoke and ash clouds above them. They are flying more or less blind, distancing themselves from Iceland at two hundred kilometers an hour.

It takes an eternal twenty minutes of suspense, sweat and steering before they clear the line of fire. To Sam's wonderment and, the best news ever, heavily veiled heavens open to show wisps of white. Clouds! Feathery clouds! He had not been aware of how much he loved the sky. Wonderful! They are coming out from beneath the ash cover. Sam lets up on the gas and elevates to three thousand feet. Piet points to the GPS instrument and compass. Both are working smoothly. Piet immediately turns the dials to emergency landing options quickly locating the Faroe Island airport, fourth on the list. The closer choices are all on Iceland, not an option.

Four hundred, seventy-nine miles, that's almost eight hundred kilometers. Sam checks the fuel gage. They have already used up a quarter tank flying full speed. To hell with it, either they make it, or they don't. On the plus side, winds are mild and when Sam aligns the Cessna with GPS coordinates, they're even at their back. That will stretch their fuel supply.

Sam presses the speaker button on the yoke, "Chicken or pasta?"

"You funky, insane fellow!" Marie shrieks, laughing and sobbing hysterically. Jace and Emma are not in much better shape as they climb over the seats to Barbu and Marie, hugging them wildly. Frenzied applause and Jace calls out, "We want champagne, damn you!" Piet raises his hand for a high-five and Sam slaps hard. Only now does he register that he is bathed in sweat. He had removed his jacket and rolled up his sleeves before starting the Cessna but, with his drenched shirt and hair, he could just as well have stepped out of a sauna. His mouth is dry as dust.

"Might there be water somewhere for the pilot?"

Emma climbs into the cockpit carrying a cooler bag. "Apparently the owners were planning a pleasure trip," she says with a wink.

The bag is filled with sandwiches and drinks. Evidently the earthquake foiled their plans. The beer cans are still cold.

"Mais c'est pas possible!" Marie shouts with glee. There are not enough beers to go around, the bag was evidently packed for only two passengers, but who cares? They share the frothy brew. Sam's portion is served with a turbulent kiss from Marie.

"Hmmm. At our momentary cruising speed, set to save fuel, we should arrive in about four and a half hours," Sam reports.

"As long as the fuel holds," Piet adds quietly, scribbling rules of three formulas on the pilot's clipboard. If his calculations, as well as the old analog gages, are accurate they should make it. But it's cutting it close, very close. Sam looks at the calculations and nods, then subtly shakes his head. They don't all need to know. It will not do them any good to spend the next four hours anticipating disaster.

"Looks good!" Piet calls. He was aiming for a casual tone, but Barbu's raised eyebrows understood differently.

They cruise smoothly, engines humming monotonously below. Sam keeps glancing back at his companions. Marie and Piet gaze sightlessly out the windows. Finally, a hiatus; a refuge. Four hours of calm to the Cessna's soothing vibration. Four hours' reprieve from the recent dread, panic and grief they endured. Still, the horror scenes replay like GIFs in their minds again and again. Emma leans on Jace. Both of them have their eyes closed, and Sam hopes they have found sleep. Sleep. Yes, he could use some of that, too. As tension seeps from his body, exhaustion takes its place.

"Think you can hold her on course?" Sam murmurs to Piet. "I can't keep my eyes open."

Piet nods heavily, taking the yoke in his hands, imagining he is tooling down the highway. It feels pretty much the same. Instead of guardrails and road markings he has a compass and GPS. The air is astonishingly calm and the Cessna purrs, engines rolling occasionally, on her course to the Faroe Islands.

Sam closes his eyes, leaning his head on the side window. Hopefully, Piet can stay awake. After coming this far, it would be a cruel irony to end up permanently bedded down in the North Atlantic Ocean, is Sam's last thought before a deep, dreamless sleep overtakes him.

"Sam, Sam, wake up! I think we are almost there," Piet calls softly, shaking Sam's shoulder.

Sam is immediately awake and follows Piet's finger to the GPS where the islands are outlined on the display. Just under twenty minutes to go. Sam turns around and finds his friends cuddled in pairs, sleeping deeply. Chuckling to himself he turns to Piet, "Thank you, co-pilot! I can't believe you didn't fall asleep!"

"How would you know?" Piet grins.

Sam punches him lightly in the arm, "Very funny. Would you wake the passengers and pre-pare the cabin for landing?"

Heavy with sleep, the foursome in the back begin to stretch back to life. Sam turns his attention to the landing procedure. No so difficult, re-ally. The Faroe airport is built for Boeings and the like, they are bound to have enough space on the landing strip. Fly into the wind, keep the tach at sixty-five knots, lower landing flaps, flip on the carburetor heater – and then simply fly down the center of the strip. Is he forgetting something? He knows he is. There must be something else. Landing gear for God's sake! He didn't have that on his single-engine jet. Did he even raise it? Sam fingers toward the switch and sees the gear locked control lamp. Piet grins broadly. Obviously, he raised the gear according to the checklist. Good thing, too, otherwise, with the landing gear out, they would have burned too much fuel, drying up far from their destination. Sam had forgotten all about it.

"Cessna on position Whiskey Alpha, identify yourself." Sam and Piet start at the sudden sound in their headphones. Piet raises both thumbs. Faroe air control! They have entered Faroe airspace! The tower has tried in vain to raise them over the usual airport radio frequencies. Judging from their flight path, outside of all regular lanes, they called on the emergency radio frequency. Sam and his friends are on the Faroe airport radar.

"This is…" Sam begins, only to realize he hasn't a clue. Piet points to the dashboard. Aha! TF-J66. Sam smiles his gratitude.

"Air control, this is tango – foxtrot – Juliette – six – six. This is an emergency flight. We request permission to land," Sam reports. Static silence and then, "Standby."

ATCO must coordinate their landing. Sam's faltering identification clued them in – he is definitely not a commercial pilot.

"Here is Vágar airport control, what is your condition?"

"We fled earthquakes and volcanos on Iceland. There are six passengers, none injured. The pilot has neither license nor experience with double-engine aircraft."

"O.K. Standby." Static.

"O.K. Juliette-six-six sink to one thousand feet and turn to sixty degrees. Can you do that?"

"Roger and wilco," Sam responds proudly. Yes, that he can do, "I copy, carrying out instructions."

"Lane sixty-five is open as is the surrounding air space. You have priority."

Sam points out the window. There it is! Faroe's westernmost island Vágar. He can already see the landing strip lights. Piet indicates the red LED on the dashboard. One of their tanks is empty and the other is in the reserve zone. The propellers are still active, but they cannot afford more than one descent. Sam will have to land on the first attempt.

He remembers his first solo landing. Only on his sixth descent had he managed to land the plane accurately. A plane he had been very familiar with, having flown it more than fifty hours all told.

"Air control Vágar! I will need landing assistance," He whispers into the mic, hoping the others won't hear him.

"Yeah, we can see that, the way you're wobbling up there" the man chuckled. "But keep calm, we're activating the VASI. You familiar with it?"

The VASI – visual approach slope indicator – is a red and white light system, indicating a plane's position upon descent. The colors change according to a plane's height, depth and center position in relation to the landing strip.

"Confirmed," Sam replies. How was that now? Red over white, you're alright;

red over red, you're dead. Right, he must fly so that the top row of lights is red and those beneath are white. Then he's all right.

"O.K. Juliette-six-six, start your approach."

Sam begins to descend toward the landing strip, he hopes. Better too low than too high, he can always speed up a bit, but braking is fatal.

Flaps in landing position, landing gear lowered. The Cessna responds kindly, like a gentle horse with an inexperienced rider. She glides calmly toward the airport, taking the course Sam intends.

"You're too far left," Piet informs him. "Now too low."

Dammit, I can see that for myself, Sam thinks. Still, he is grateful not to be alone up here in the cockpit. He has enough to do keeping tabs on speed and elevation.

"You seem to be all right. Good luck!" Faroe tower offers. Very funny! Sam is not amused. But he seems to be doing it right after all. All red on top, all white underneath. Fifty more meters and they will be on the ground. What now? The top left lights are now white, and the bottom center lights are red. What does it mean? Sam is lost, grinning his stress-grin.

"Nose down, nose down," his Avionic system instructs him calmly over the headphones. Sam dips the Cessna's nose. Twenty meters, ten, five. He pulls the fuel lever completely back and lets the plane glide. Stall warnings beep in his ears when he dares to lift the vessel's nose a touch. The wheels squeal as they hit tarmac. Perfect landing! Don't get distracted now, he tells himself, concentrate! They speed down the strip at a hundred kilometers an hour. Sam focuses on holding the plane firmly in line. One false move and a gust of wind could send them back up or cause them to weave and capsize. With rotating lights and howling sirens, fire engines approach rapidly on both sides. Sam carefully presses the brakes and the plane comes to a halt. They're way off-center, on the far left of the strip. Still, they're down and safe on the first attempt!

Sam's head sinks onto the dashboard. The right door is wrenched open to reveal a fireman in full gear at the top of a debarking ramp. On the steps behind him, foam extinguishers are aimed like machine guns at the small aircraft. Piet automatically raises his hands when he moves to the door, raising a grin on the headman's face. The firemen clear the way. Piet takes the steps slowly, wondering which events had been the dream and which are reality. He is followed by Marie, Barbu, Emma and Jace, their faces reflecting similar befuddlement. When everyone else has debarked, Sam leaves the cockpit and takes the steps. He is immediately encased in a ten-arm bear hug. Flashbulbs pop, startling them out of their collective cuddle. Evidently, the press was also listening to emergency frequencies.

They are led to a bus and driven to the terminal. Sam is shocked when he sees his image in a mirror next to the terminal entrance. They look like war refugees, their filthy clothes and soot-blackened faces. Piet fishes his cellphone out. Time for a selfie! Barbu places the backpack with the stones behind him, well out of sight. He has a hunch it could mean trouble.

A uniformed officer brings them to a spacious room at the end of the airport lobby. Both plainclothes and uniformed police, white-jacketed doctors and other rescue services look up when they arrive. Despite how they look, it is evident that they are not in need of immediate medical attention. Faroe Island authorities have been expecting refugees from Iceland since yesterday. Any boat they could spare has been sent out on evacuation missions. Sam's group is one of the first to make it to Vágar, and the only one by plane, preceded only by a couple of Icelandic trawlers and their crews whose main purpose was to coordinate rescues. Since yesterday, however, no lack of journalists from all over the world have been pouring in to get as close as possible to events as they unfold.

After assuring the doctors that they are fine, the police take over. They are very considerate, supplying them with drinks and giving them a moment to catch their breath. One policewoman introduces herself as Freika and seems to be supervising activities. She instructs her colleagues to take each of them to a separate desk and document their statements, waving Sam into her office.

"Well then, you were very lucky to get out of Iceland at all. Your methods were rather risky, I must admit, but you landed safely," she begins. "The situation on Iceland is cataclysmic. The last radio communication or telephone call we received was hours ago and we can't seem to raise anyone from our end. You are the first to make it here. Two hours ago, a private jet was detected floating in the ocean not far from the coast. The engines failed. No wonder, really, flying through the ash clouds. We don't know yet if there are survivors. You were smart to fly beneath them."

Bruna! That must be Bruna and Pedro's jet. Sam merely nods, not sure if he should mention that he knows them or if it's better to hold his tongue.

Freika enters his personal data into her computer. Like all of them, he hasn't any ID with him. She tells him they will forward their data to the closest embassies who will then inform their relatives. The embassies will supply them with fresh passports, and they can soon continue on their way home. Here, Freika hesitates, "The Cessna is registered in Sten Lagergrön's name, a Swedish citizen. Do you know him?"

"To be honest…" Sam begins reluctantly, "We just took it. We couldn't find anyone at the airport, and we needed to get out of there. Katla was about to erupt."

Freika looks at him in amazement, waiting for him to continue.

"And I don't have a valid pilot's license, either," Sam finishes.

"Then it's more than a miracle that you made it so far. However, we will have to decide how to deal with the theft and air rights infringements."

TWELVE

S am sits down with his coffee in the lobby. They have been given rooms in a small bed & breakfast. The owner, Guðrun, is a stocky woman with untamable strawberry blond hair. When they stepped in the door, she took each of them in her arms, tears welling up in her eyes. Both of her sons work in Reykjavik. Day before yesterday, she said good-bye, not expecting to see them again for a few days. But they always call daily. She has not heard from them since yesterday morning. Plagued with worry, until she has definite news one way or the other, she will keep herself busy with the six survivors she just adopted.

Their luck is almost spooky. They were ferried from Vágar airport to the eastern neighbor Streymoy, home to Faroe Islands capital city, Tórshavn. Bed & breakfasts and hotels are scarce in the tiny city, yet they receive rooms. The police were kind enough to hustle them out of the terminal and into waiting cars, so the six survivors were spared media madness. But it won't be long before they turn up here, Sam thinks, it's a small world up here. In preparation for larger groups of refugees, beds, cots and heating elements are being installed in warehouses, schools and other public facilities. International aid has already arrived and set up their equipment to treat the wounded. The entire population is rising to help their neighbors. Homes are flung open, offering beds for those not in need of close medical attention, much to the relief of the makeshift medical facilities. Mountains of blankets, food, clothing and even children's toys are donated and distributed among the refugee centers. Solidarity and compassion are written in capital letters.

Marie turns up in what Sam calls the lobby but is actually more like a cozy living room. There's an open fireplace, some period furniture with crocheted doilies and the walls are nearly completely obscured by family photos. It feels like a visit to Grandma's. Marie is wearing a bathrobe and has a terrycloth turban holding up her hair. Guðrun lent Sam, Jace, Piet and Barbu clothes from her sons, but had nothing for the ladies. The good woman generously offered to give them some of her own clothes, but Emma and Marie did not want to deplete her meager wardrobe and happily chose from the abundant, in both senses of the word, selection of men's clothes until their own are washed and repaired. Marie and Sam share a room, Jace and Emma another and Barbu and Piet another. They fill half of the b & b's capacity.

Marie settles on the arm of Sam's time-worn easy chair and presses his head to her side. She closes her eyes and holds him there, while he gazes up at her face.

"We're safe. We made it out…" Sam whispers hoarsely. Marie nods and begins to tremble. Sam pulls her onto his lap, and she begins to cry, tears flowing down her cheeks and onto Sam's hands. He pulls her even closer, stroking her neck and feels warmth rising to his face and his own tears mingle with hers.

"I just can't stop thinking about all the people on Iceland, about our friends, about Jon," she says when the salty river becomes a trickle. They are nose-to-nose, and her dark, red-rimmed eyes look directly into his. Sam presses a gentle kiss on her lips as if he could thusly cover her grief and trauma. At first, Marie merely accepts the kiss, but then she begins to respond. Like a woman dying of thirst, she can only take in a few drops at a time until her body and mind are ready to drink an ocean.

An "Oho!" behind them interrupts the moment and Marie extricates herself from Sam's arms, sliding back onto the arm of the chair. Jace and Emma are standing a few steps away, Barbu and Piet are leaning in the door frame.

"What?" Marie demands with a smile.

"We just weren't sure how far that was going to go," Emma replies.

Marie gives Emma the once-over and cannot suppress a giggle. Emma is wearing burgundy corduroys at least six sizes too large and held up with a piece of rope around her hips. The ensemble is completed with a blue and white flannel shirt, size XL. "Is that available in my size?"

Emma blushes and spins around, "Do you really think it suits me? It cost a fortune!"

Grinning, Barbu and Piet plop down on the sofa. Jace and Emma occupy the other easy chair. On the men, Guðrun's son's clothes may be baggy here and there, but none of them are swimming in them. Emma chose the clothes over a massive bathrobe. Marie is wearing Guðrun's. Emma decides it makes no difference whether it was the disaster or other natural causes that brought Marie and the much older Sam together. She wishes them all the best.

Jace picks up the remote from the side table and turns on the TV. Zapping through the channels until he finds CNN. Breaking News in large red letters repeats itself on the crawler beneath the newswoman. They all snap to attention and Jace turns up the volume.

We still have little information on the current situation on Iceland. Apparently, a volcano beneath Langjökull glacier, not far from the capital Reykjavik, erupted yesterday. The eruption triggered a massive ice and mud avalanche which crashed into the ocean, which in turn brought about a tidal wave that has evidently demolished a greater part of the city. Further destruction was caused by an additional eruption later the same day. The volcano Katla, one of Iceland's largest, violently erupted, hurling large masses of liquid magma up to fifty kilometers distant over the island and coastal waters. The ash cloud has now reached the stratosphere, bringing eternal dusk to Iceland during its short summer season. Little is known as to the number of fatalities, but current estimates assume one hundred thousand people have lost their lives or will soon die of gas poisoning or in fires. The newscaster is obviously shaken.

Videos taken from a military helicopter flying low over the water along the coast appear on the screen. They see what's left of Vik, with Katla angrily spewing lava and ash in the background.

They see Reykjavik's devastated shore and the northern Old City that looks as if it had been fire-bombed, viciously and repeatedly. Only the part behind the hill where the cathedral and inland air-port are located show moderate damage, as well as a few of the suburbs. Everywhere, fires are raging, and it is obvious that the firefighters are hopelessly overtaxed.

"Mon Dieu," Marie whispers into her hand pressed against her mouth.

"A hundred thousand…that's a third of the population! It's a bloody massacre," Jace murmurs. The others simply stare at the TV, their faces rigid as stone.

International aid and British military are entering Faroe harbors as we speak. U.S. American, Canadian and other European fleets are also underway carrying food, drinking water and emergency rescue facilities. Within the next hours, military troops will support British aid organizations, who are the first to arrive at the scene of the disaster. NATO officers, acting for the European Union, will assume command of coordinating rescue missions.

Updates inform us that the entire airspace over Europe and as far as Moscow is now closed to civilian air traffic. Meteorologists predict that the ash clouds will move southeast over the European continent in the next few hours.

We now have contact with our special reporter Ted Markholm who is coming to us from Tórshavn, capital city of the Faroe Islands, eight hundred kilometers southeast of Iceland. What can you tell us, Ted?

Thank you, Nancy. It's true, at the moment there is little to go on. We have learned that British military aid will establish their headquarters at the Faroe airport with the Danish government's full support. At Keflavik airport, forty kilometers from Reykjavik, attempts have been made to fly out survivors. However, Keflavik is located at Iceland's westernmost tip and the ash cloud prohibits flying civilian aircraft in or out of the airport. There is a small marina in Keflavik and ships will attempt to evacuate from there, providing emergency medical treatment. Survivors are also using the nearly intact Ring Road. On foot or in busses, they head North in hopes of finding safety there. The number of fatalities can only be surmised but is certainly in the tens of thousands and it's anybody's guess how many are wounded, buried or trapped beneath the rubble. Communication is practically non-existent and still-functioning cell-phone masts are reserved for official communications. However, an amateur volcanologist has managed to transmit images of Reykjavik via satellite and social media networks.

Ted Markholm is reporting from Tórshavn Harbor, and they can see numerous freight ships laying in the water and large military transport helicopters flying over the screen behind him.

Let's get to that later, Ted. What can you tell us about the people on Iceland?

"Jon!" Piet and Barbu say simultaneously. The crazy bugger actually managed to contact the outside world with his makeshift satellite and car battery. Sam lays his finger on his lips and points at the screen.

As I said, Nancy, there is little or no information about current conditions on Iceland. Naturally, everything humanly possible is being done to ensure help reaches disaster survivors. What we can say is the eruptions have wrought havoc no less devastating than the atomic bombs dropped in World War II and its repercussions are impossible to foresee. Experts warn that Katla's ash clouds will not only paralyze air traffic for months to come but will also eclipse the sun for weeks, causing unsurpassed and unpredictable damage to Nature and farmland. Economic prognoses are competing for the direst horror scenario and we could be looking at another global market crisis. As Ted ended his report, a wobbly, blurred video, obviously recorded with a mobile phone, took the screen. The video was shot from Hallgrímskirkja's balcony, looking down through swathes of black smoke on the wreckage once known as Reykjavik. Crowds of milling people can be made out, but not much else. The grainy, smudged quality of the images only underscores their apocalyptic atmosphere.

We interrupt our report for a word from our sponsors. The TV erupted in shrilly laughing children hopping eagerly around a smiling mother passing out chocolate bars. Healthy snacks for strong children chanted a cheerful woman's voice. Jace pushes the mute button.

"The video is from Jon," Emma comments, breaking the oppressive silence.

"It looks like he got his scoop. Do you think Chuck made it, too?" Marie wonders.

"For sure, Chuck's indestructible," Piet states firmly.

"We could try to call him," Barbu suggests, pulling his battered cellphone from his pocket.

"No reception. Or the Iceland card doesn't reach this far," he says, disappointed.

"Even if it did, you heard them, the communications system isn't working. But we can try to send him a message with a computer. Then he will know where to find us when he turns up," Sam replies, indicating an elderly PC for guests' use on the quaint rolltop desk.

"Mon Dieu," Marie interjects fitfully, "I am still expecting to wake up and find out this was all a horrible dream. It is incredible to think that only a few hours ago we were going about our lives, guiding obnoxious tourists through Silfra's cold waters. And now so many are dead! Their lives snuffed out within seconds! Smashed, burned, drowned or buried beneath the rubble, waiting to be rescued and dying slow, torturous deaths!"

Her words blanket them all in stunned silence. They exchange looks out of horrified eyes. Emma begins to cry and stumbles to Marie. They meet in an embrace, both sobbing uncontrollably. Sam gets up and hugs two of them close. Jace, Piet and Barbu gravitate to the trio, wrapping their arms around them all. They stand there in the middle of the room, holding each other as if they were drowning and this is how Guðrun finds them when she brings in a tray laden with sandwiches. She places the tray on a table and spreads her meaty arms around them all. She is overcome with grief for them, for her still missing sons and the horrors her guests have been through and her sons are probably still experiencing. Anxiety over-whelms her, and she begins to cry loudly, giving them the space and permission to melt their fro-zen hearts, here and now, safe in her home. Barbu grieves openly for his brother, Sam for Ian, Marie for Ilias, Piet mourns the destruction of Silfra's maj-esty, Emma and Jace grieve for the beauty they shared where they found each other and fell in love. Each of them weeps for their personal losses and for the devastation they have miraculously sur-vived.

After a time, their tears and sobs subside. Una-shamed, they dive into the wonderful sandwiches. Their throats are clear, their hearts relieved, their minds at rest for the moment.

"A man from the police station was here. You are to report to the German embassy here in Tórshavn as soon as possible. They will be han-dling communications with your homelands," Guðrun informs them, happy to see them eating so heartily. It's a good sign. She hasn't eaten since the day before yesterday. "By the way, your clothes are in your rooms."

They thank her profusely for her kindness.

Back in their b & b, Sam expresses his relief, "That went better than I thought it would."

They had gone to the German consulate together and discovered it would only be a couple of days before they would all have emergency passports and money to tide them over. Only the Romanian Embassy would need more time to attend to Barbu but the British passports for Jace and Emma, French for Marie, Dutch for Piet and Swiss for Sam were all underway. Sam was required to make a statement with the local police regarding the 'borrowed' Cessna and air rights infringements but whether charges would be pressed remained to be seen. After that, they would be free to take a ferry to England and from there return to their homelands.

"Man, can you imagine? Five hundred euros apiece!" Piet laughs and slaps Barbu on the back, "Except for you, my friend."

Barbu takes it in stride, remarking, "Yes, but while you all were busy becoming shooting stars

on the media heavens, I did something useful."
Barbu is referring to the BBC team they had run
into on the way back from the embassy. Judging
by their clothes, stature and the building they had
just left, lurking journalists suspected they were
Iceland survivors and cornered them, pressing for
an interview. For the most part, it was Jace and
Sam who recounted their experiences with the
earthquake and eruption at Langjökull, giving an
account of their race against the lahar in the jeep
and their final flight to the Faroe Islands. Barbu
was damned if his family would hear of his
brother's death on television. Besides, what could
he tell the reporters? That his brother fell to his
death trying to hold onto a diamond the size of a
softball? Not a chance. But Simi was one of the
earthquake's first victims, how could he recount
his experiences without mentioning him? Impossible. And he was not going to lie, either. So, he
took his pain and slipped away. His heart ached
for his family. He had to tell them, face to face. His
parents would be devastated. He knew it was un-
founded but being the elder he felt an insidious
guilt at not being able to save his younger
brother. He longed for his family to absolve him,
which he knew they would. He also needed to decide what to tell them. They will want details.

Clever questions and bright camera lights seduced the others into telling all. Marie expressly wanted Jon's name mentioned as a true hero, but it would probably be edited out. Fortunately, they had the presence of mind to keep quiet about the diamonds. Sam also got a bit of a story from the journalists: Several severely injured passengers were rescued from the ditched jet and brought to a hospital frigate via ambulance helicopter. Sam sincerely hoped Bruna was among them.

Barbu opens the paper bag he is carrying and places letter scales on the table.

"What's that?" Piet asks. Everyone else knows immediately.

Sam rises from the easy chair and gives a nod. They all troop up the stairs to his and Marie's room. The scales are placed on the floor and Barbu retrieves the backpack from his room.

After an hour of sorting and weighing, they have four piles of stones. Jace reads back to them the calculations on his notepad.

"We have two stones each weighing slightly over one thousand grams; seventeen stones at about two hundred grams each; fifty stones at more or less one hundred grams each and six hundred eighty-four stones between four and forty grams apiece," he reports, adding, "Do you have any idea what that means?"

Five questioning faces reply.

"I'm no expert, but I do know a bit from my cousin. He's a gemmologist working for one the biggest dealers in London and Zurich."

"And that means?" Marie demands.

"Well, when these really are raw diamonds, we are sitting on immense wealth, though their worth varies greatly depending on how big and how pure they are," Jace tells them.

Circling his finger in diver's speak, Sam asks him to keep going.

"That means…" he says, tapping the notated numbers into his cellphone calculator, "once the stones are cut, we can reckon with forty percent net weight. That's a whopping fifty thousand carats. But, like I said, their worth depends on their purity and size."

"I still don't understand," Marie interjects.

"Let me give you an example. The largest diamond ever found is the Cullinan. The Cullinan was found in 1905 near Pretoria, South Africa and weighed three thousand and six carats. Internet tells us that the raw diamond was used to produce the Great Star of Africa and the Second Star of Africa, both now part of the British Crown Jewels. The most valuable cut diamond, the Oppenheimer Blue, weighs only fourteen and a half carats. It was sold in Geneva in 2016 for more than fifty-seven million dollars."

"And we have two stones weighing more than a kilo?" Emma exclaims, her voice husky.

"One carat is 0.2 grams. You have to remember that cutting pares away forty percent of a raw diamond. That adds up to…" he punches numbers on the mobile, "about four thousand carats for both of the largest ones, when they're cut."

Marie stretches out her upturned hand, thumb, pointer and middle finger brought together. How much? Jace runs the fingers of his left hand through his hair again and again while tapping numbers with his right thumb on the cellphone. His eyes widen and seem huge when he looks up and meets their expectant gaze.

"If my calculations are right, it adds up to a hundred million U.S. dollars or more per stone!"

Jace's bulging eyes stare into five open mouths.

"What the fuck!" Emma breathes. They look at each other, stunned, and then all hell breaks loose. They shout and shriek at the top of their voices.

"Stop, stop, stop!" Jace hollers, trying to calm them down. "For God's sake, shut up! Do you want everyone in town to know what's up? Jeez! I told I don't know much about it. We do not even know if these really are raw diamonds. And if they are, we haven't the slightest idea how pure they are or what they're worth!"

The ensuing stunned silence is of another sort altogether.

Sam is the first to find his voice again, "If I get you right, we might all be millionaires. But we could just as easily have weighed a pile of pebbles. Yeah?"

Jace nods.

"Then we should find out what we've got."

"How do you suggest we go about doing that?" Barbu asks, the only one beside Sam that has kept his cool.

"We should photograph the stones and send them along with a few stones to Jace's cousin, and he can tell us what's what," Sam replies.

Jace gets practical, "My cousin and his family live in London. We all know how difficult it is to travel right now. More and more refugees are coming from Iceland, the warehouses are jam-packed and so are the ferries to England. I don't know where all of us can stay in London, my flat is miniscule. How should we go about it?"

"You're right. But we can send you with the pictures and a few stones. The rest of us can go to my place in Switzerland and wait for you there. I have got plenty of room and, it seems the chaos has yet to hit Switzerland as hard as the rest of Europe," Sam suggests.

Naturally, the ash clouds have hit Switzerland as well, but as opposed to other countries, the Swiss are well-prepared. Since the end of WWI, the Swiss have invested billions of francs in national security. During the Cold War, the Swiss Civilian Organization requested each household to store enough emergency rations for two weeks. The army's mandatory stores held, and still hold, enough vital medicines, fuels and foodstuffs to sustain the entire population for months. The butt of many a joke, in recent years the concept has been challenged due to its high maintenance and cost. Not any longer. The Swiss caution, what some might call paranoia, is paying off without the added drama of war being waged. While other European countries are battling to counteract food shortages, looting, closed banks protecting their insufficient cash from panicking and furious citizens, long ration lines, roads blocked with traffic, and electricity outages, the Swiss are going about their daily lives with enough to eat, smoothly running public transportation, medical attention and patrolling military to maintain order. Nonetheless, the government has issued emergency level one and rationing of certain goods. Understandably, the stock market has been closed for the duration.

"I need to get home as soon as possible," Barbu announces, looking around at each of them. They nod their understanding. Barbu needs to bring the news of Simi's death to his family.

Shortly thereafter, they plug in three bedtable lamps and take photos of some of the larger stones with Sam's cellphone, showing the individual weights on a slip of paper laid beside the corresponding stone. They sort out a selection for John, Jace's cousin to examine, choosing three of each group of smaller stones and the smaller of the large ones. The rest is packed in paper and returned to the backpack. They then upload the photos onto one of Sam's cloud files using Guðrun's house computer.

Three weeks have passed since they arrived in Tórshavn and just this morning they received their emergency passports and funds from the German embassy. Barbu is still waiting for his and it may be some time before he can travel home to his parents.

"What are you thinking about?" Sam asks Marie, gently caressing her cheek.

They are back in their room, lounging on the bed. Having received their passports and emergency funds, they all pitched in and invited Guðrun to dinner at a small harbor restaurant. It was a small way of saying thank you after all she had done for them. Besides, she had reason to celebrate. Her sons had survived the disaster, but only just. Both were in the hospital, one with severe burns, the other with several broken bones. But they would heal, the doctors assured her. At first, she balked at the expense, but they finally convinced her to join them. The food was excellent, and they were happy to see Guðrun tuck in heartily. It was a lovely evening.

"Why?" What do you mean?" Marie asks back.

"We'll be on our way out of here tomorrow and I would think that's a good thing, but you don't seem particularly happy about it."

"My thoughts keep bouncing back and forth. One minute I'm imaging all the things I can do as a rich woman, the next, I'm back on Iceland, reliving the horrors and thinking of all those poor people and the chaos there and all over Europe."

"Yeah, things won't be business as usual for some time to come. Still, it's not getting worse. Katla has settled down over the last couple of days and the ash cloud is moving northwards," Sam offers his meager solace.

Marie has to chuckle and kisses him lightly, "You men are all alike, aren't you? Everything under control, right?"

"No, of course not. But we will get it under control. And what about us?"

"What about us? We're going to buy an island, have twelve children and start a new tribe," Marie decides.

"Hm" Sam rumbles and takes her into his arms. Marie yawns and snuggles in close to his warmth.

Have they really hit the mother lode? Sam feels distinctly uncomfortable at the thought of being immeasurably rich. He knows how drastically wealth can change a person, and it's rarely for the good. Feeling Marie's heavy warmth beside him, he wonders about their future together. What began as a simple affair, at least for her, has been welded by volcanic fires, hardened by tidal waves and their harrowing miraculous escape. But just how strong is their bond? A chill sprints through his blood when he thinks of her waking up one day, in the ho-hum of business as usual and realizing she's tethered herself to an old man. It occurs to him that he knows neither her age nor her birthday. Tomorrow, he will ask her.

Additional books by Stefan Prebil

LORENA – 2032 Die Zeit der Wahrheit

Paperback ISBN: 978-3-7497-2629-5
Hardcover ISBN: 978-3-7497-2650-9
e-Book ISBN: 978-3-7497-2651-6
Hörbuch: ISBN 978-3-033-06774-5

English Version in January 2020

Summary

LORENA - 2032 The Time of Truth

It is 2032: Jacko Brevic approaches the age of 70 and prepares to approach immortality through a self-experiment. Despite his advanced age, he still hasn't had enough of life.

But then his unintentionally pregnant granddaughter confronts him with his nondigested past: the adoption release of her father.
As a result, a momentous fraud of his former friend comes to light, which, apart from Jacko, also plunges the entire Swiss society into a dilemma

Zeitfracht Medien GmbH
Ferdinand-Jühlke-Straße 7
99095 Erfurt, Deutschland
produktsicherheit@kolibri360.de